STONE ARCH BOOKS
a capstone imprint

◥◤ STONE ARCH BOOKS™

Published in 2014 by Stone Arch Books
A Capstone Imprint
1710 Roe Crest Drive
North Mankato, MN 56003
www.capstonepub.com

Originally published by DC Comics in the U.S. in single
magazine form as Batman: Li'l Gotham.
Copyright © 2014 DC Comics. All Rights Reserved.

DC Comics
1700 Broadway, New York, NY 10019
A Warner Bros. Entertainment Company

Printed in China.
032014   008085LEOF14

Cataloging-in-Publication Data is available at the Library
of Congress website:
ISBN: 978-1-4342-9219-3 (library binding)

Summary: As Gotham City begins to celebrate St.
Patrick's Day, the banks discover that there's no gold left
under the rainbow. Batman and his crew round up the
usual green-eyed goons in pursuit of the missing money,
but no good deed goes unpunished... Then, on Easter,
Batman and Robin are late for a very important date: the
Mad Hatter is terrorizing all of Gotham with every ounce
of his egg-splosive fury!

STONE ARCH BOOKS
Ashley C. Andersen Zantop **Publisher**
Michael Dahl **Editorial Director**
Sean Tulien **Editor**
Heather Kindseth **Creative Director**
Bob Lentz **Art Director**
Hilary Wacholz **Designer**
Kathy McColley **Production Specialist**

DC Comics
Sarah Gaydos **Original U.S. Editor**

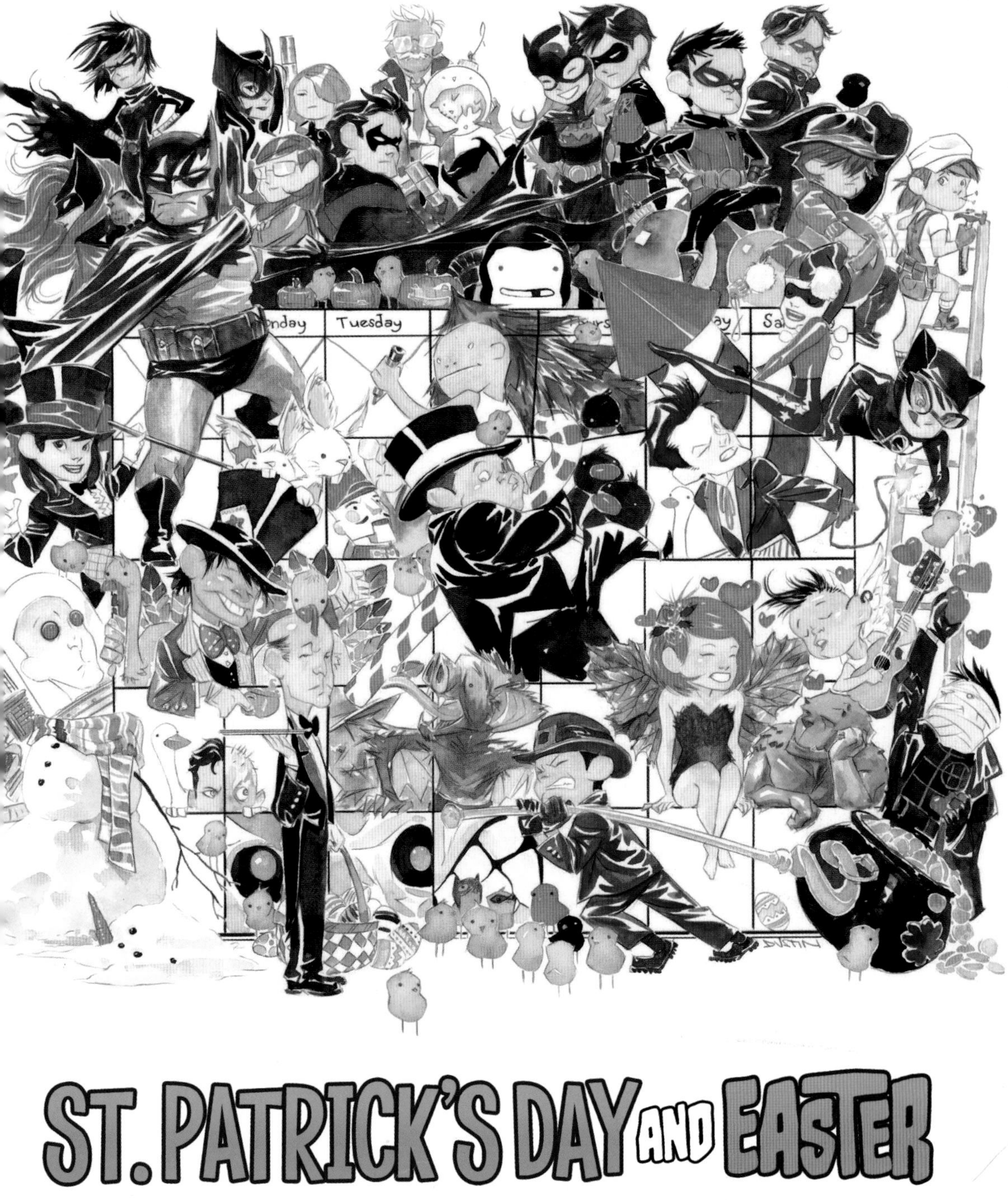
Tuesday

ST. PATRICK'S DAY AND EASTER

Dustin Nguyen & Derek Fridolfs...................... writers
Dustin Nguyen... artist
Saida Temofonte.. letterer

BATMAN created by
Bob Kane

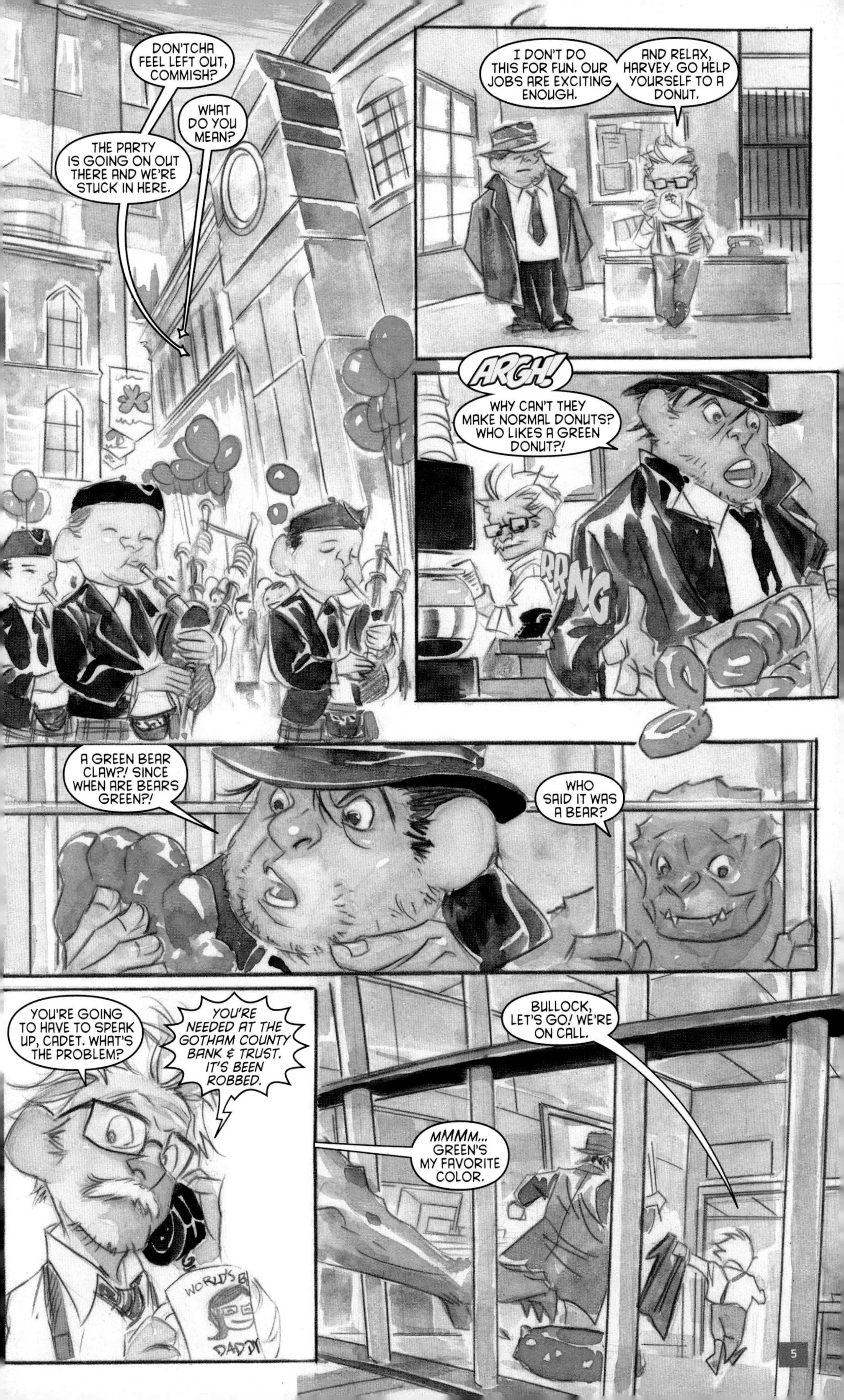
DON'TCHA FEEL LEFT OUT, COMMISH?
THE PARTY IS GOING ON OUT THERE AND WE'RE STUCK IN HERE.
WHAT DO YOU MEAN?
I DON'T DO THIS FOR FUN. OUR JOBS ARE EXCITING ENOUGH.
AND RELAX, HARVEY. GO HELP YOURSELF TO A DONUT.
ARGH!
WHY CAN'T THEY MAKE NORMAL DONUTS? WHO LIKES A GREEN DONUT?!
RRRNG
A GREEN BEAR CLAW?! SINCE WHEN ARE BEARS GREEN?!
WHO SAID IT WAS A BEAR?
YOU'RE GOING TO HAVE TO SPEAK UP, CADET. WHAT'S THE PROBLEM?
YOU'RE NEEDED AT THE GOTHAM COUNTY BANK & TRUST. IT'S BEEN ROBBED.
BULLOCK, LET'S GO! WE'RE ON CALL.
MMMM... GREEN'S MY FAVORITE COLOR.
WORLD'S B
DADDY

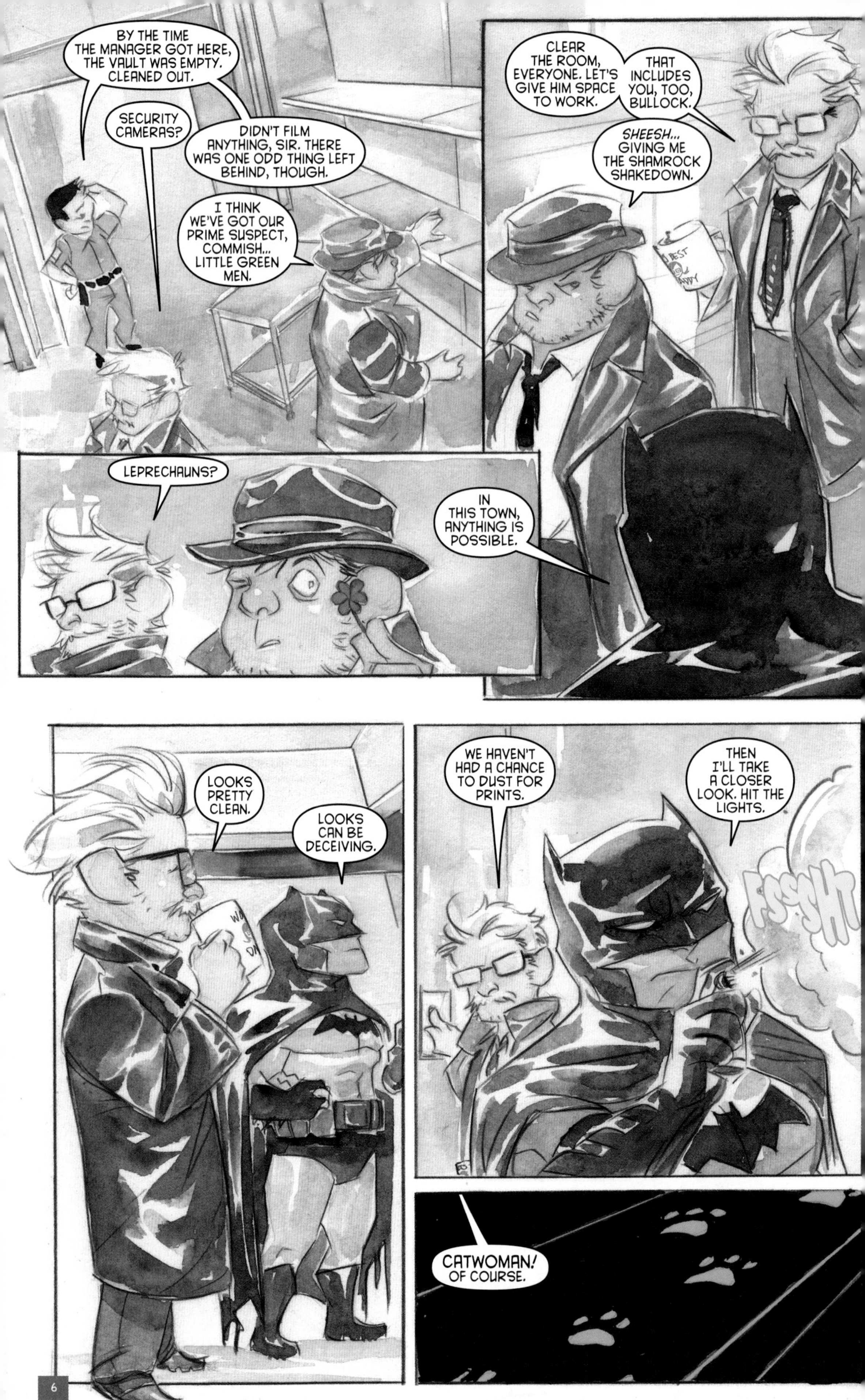
BY THE TIME THE MANAGER GOT HERE, THE VAULT WAS EMPTY. CLEANED OUT.
SECURITY CAMERAS?
DIDN'T FILM ANYTHING, SIR. THERE WAS ONE ODD THING LEFT BEHIND, THOUGH.
I THINK WE'VE GOT OUR PRIME SUSPECT, COMMISH... LITTLE GREEN MEN.
LEPRECHAUNS?
CLEAR THE ROOM, EVERYONE. LET'S GIVE HIM SPACE TO WORK.
THAT INCLUDES YOU, TOO, BULLOCK.
SHEESH... GIVING ME THE SHAMROCK SHAKEDOWN.
IN THIS TOWN, ANYTHING IS POSSIBLE.
LOOKS PRETTY CLEAN.
LOOKS CAN BE DECEIVING.
WE HAVEN'T HAD A CHANCE TO DUST FOR PRINTS.
THEN I'LL TAKE A CLOSER LOOK. HIT THE LIGHTS.
FSSSHT
CATWOMAN! OF COURSE.

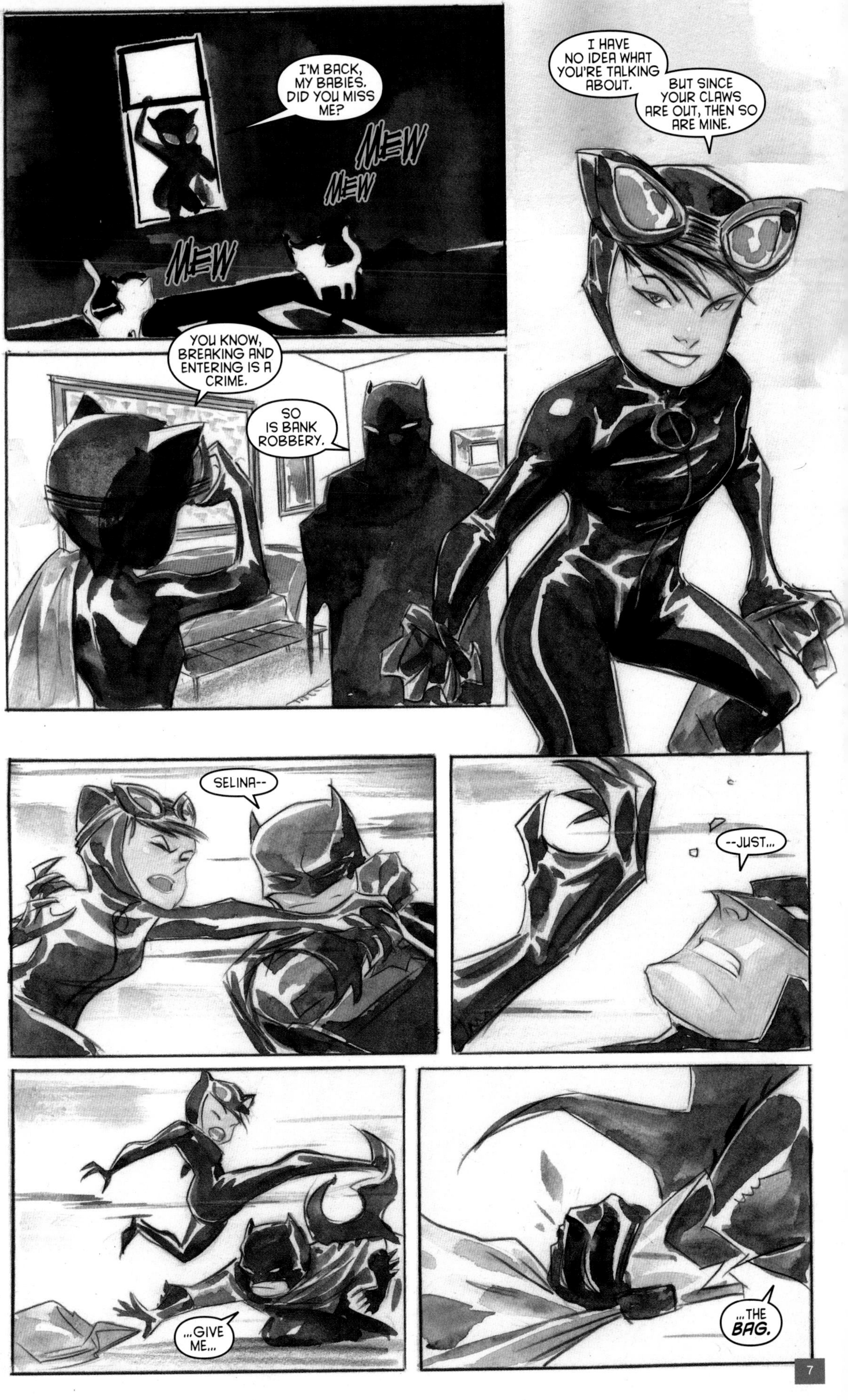
I'M BACK, MY BABIES. DID YOU MISS ME?
MEW
MEW
MEW
I HAVE NO IDEA WHAT YOU'RE TALKING ABOUT.
BUT SINCE YOUR CLAWS ARE OUT, THEN SO ARE MINE.
YOU KNOW, BREAKING AND ENTERING IS A CRIME.
SO IS BANK ROBBERY.
SELINA--
--JUST...
...GIVE ME...
...THE BAG.

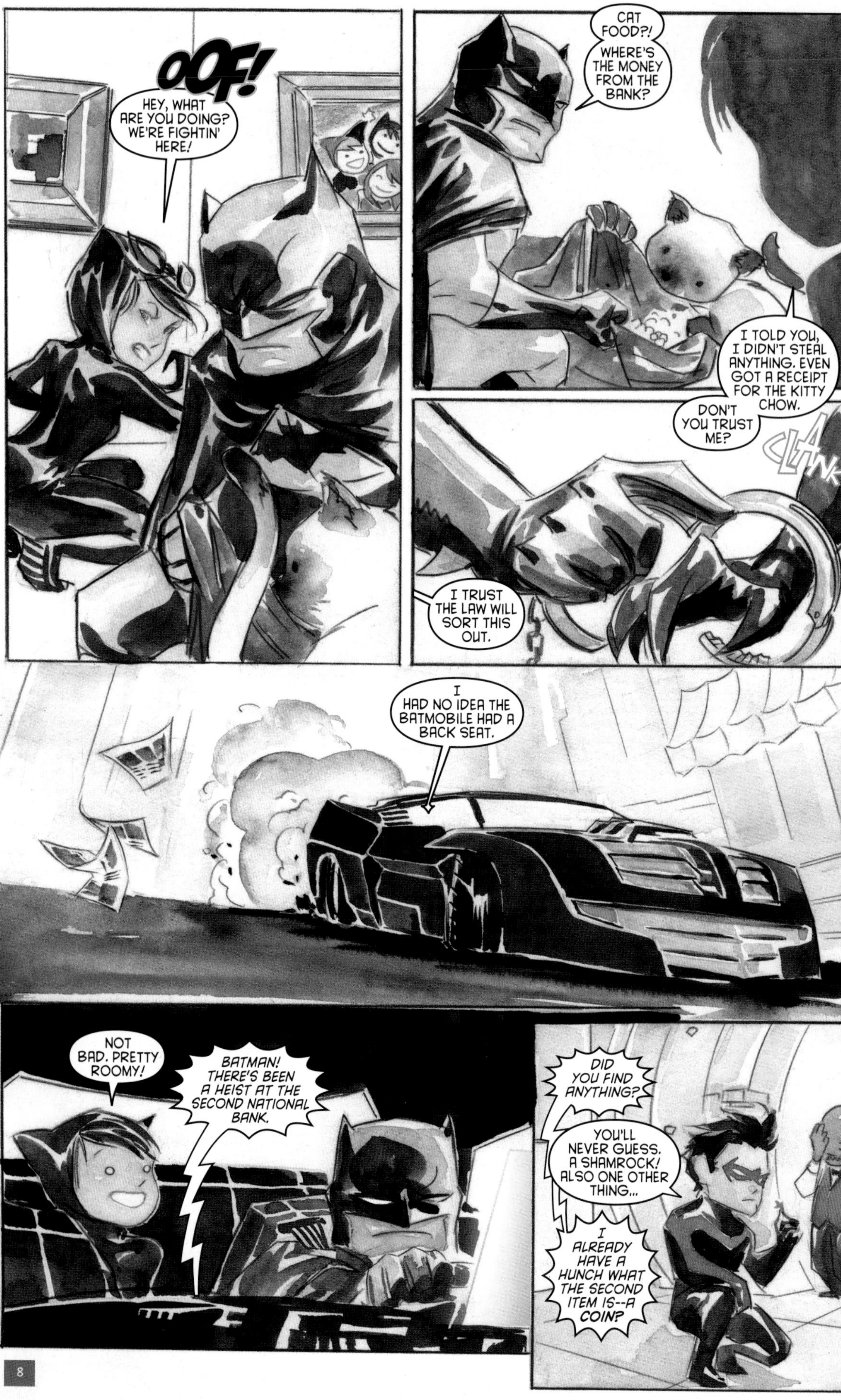
OOF!
HEY, WHAT ARE YOU DOING? WE'RE FIGHTIN' HERE!
CAT FOOD?! WHERE'S THE MONEY FROM THE BANK?
I TOLD YOU, I DIDN'T STEAL ANYTHING. EVEN GOT A RECEIPT FOR THE KITTY CHOW.
DON'T YOU TRUST ME?
CLANK
I TRUST THE LAW WILL SORT THIS OUT.
I HAD NO IDEA THE BATMOBILE HAD A BACK SEAT.
NOT BAD. PRETTY ROOMY!
BATMAN! THERE'S BEEN A HEIST AT THE SECOND NATIONAL BANK.
DID YOU FIND ANYTHING?
YOU'LL NEVER GUESS. A SHAMROCK! ALSO ONE OTHER THING...
I ALREADY HAVE A HUNCH WHAT THE SECOND ITEM IS--A COIN?

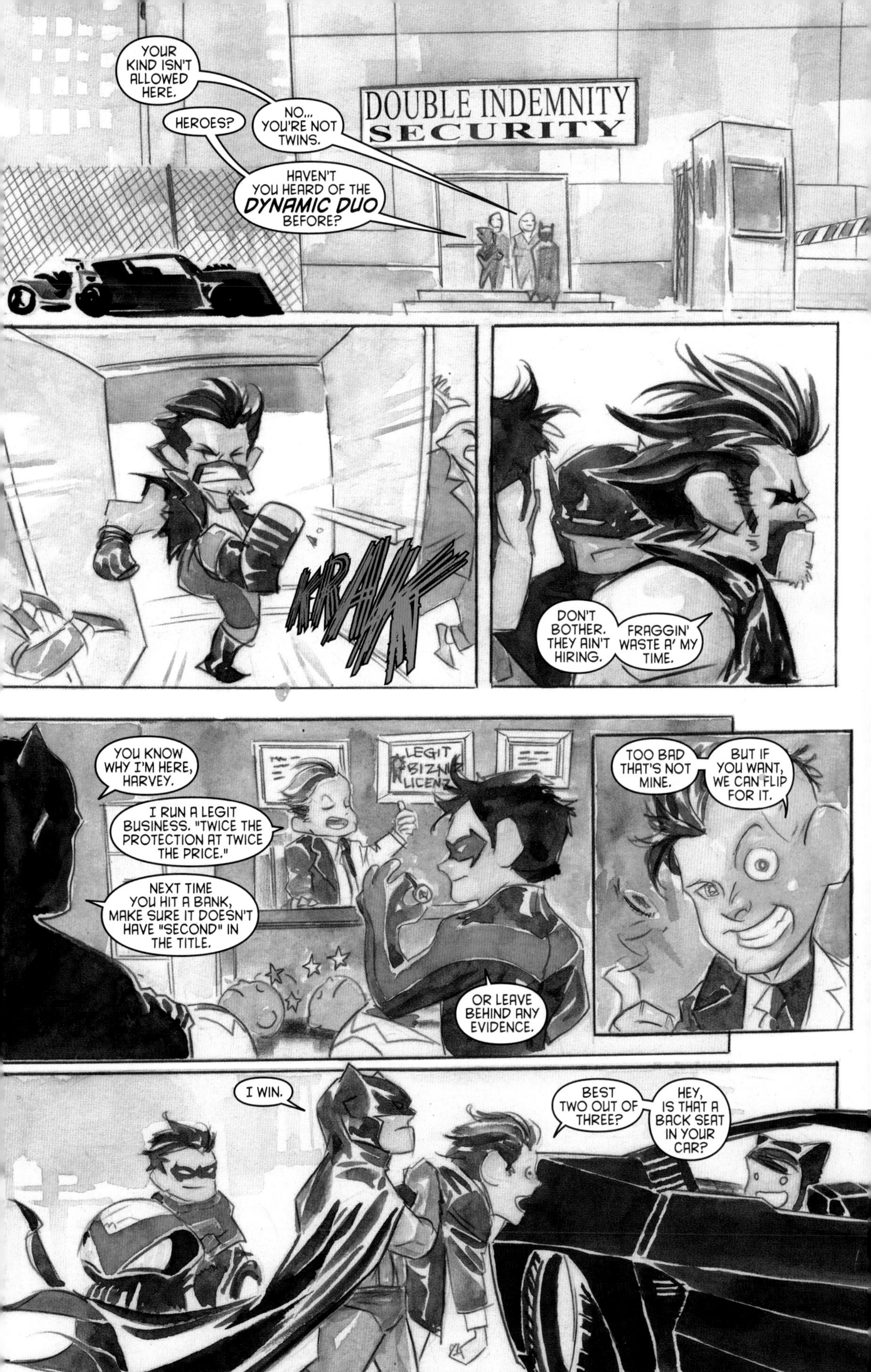
YOUR KIND ISN'T ALLOWED HERE.
NO... YOU'RE NOT TWINS.
HEROES?
HAVEN'T YOU HEARD OF THE DYNAMIC DUO BEFORE?
DOUBLE INDEMNITY SECURITY
KRAAK
DON'T BOTHER. THEY AIN'T HIRING.
FRAGGIN' WASTE A' MY TIME.
YOU KNOW WHY I'M HERE, HARVEY.
I RUN A LEGIT BUSINESS. "TWICE THE PROTECTION AT TWICE THE PRICE."
NEXT TIME YOU HIT A BANK, MAKE SURE IT DOESN'T HAVE "SECOND" IN THE TITLE.
OR LEAVE BEHIND ANY EVIDENCE.
TOO BAD THAT'S NOT MINE.
BUT IF YOU WANT, WE CAN FLIP FOR IT.
I WIN.
BEST TWO OUT OF THREE?
HEY, IS THAT A BACK SEAT IN YOUR CAR?

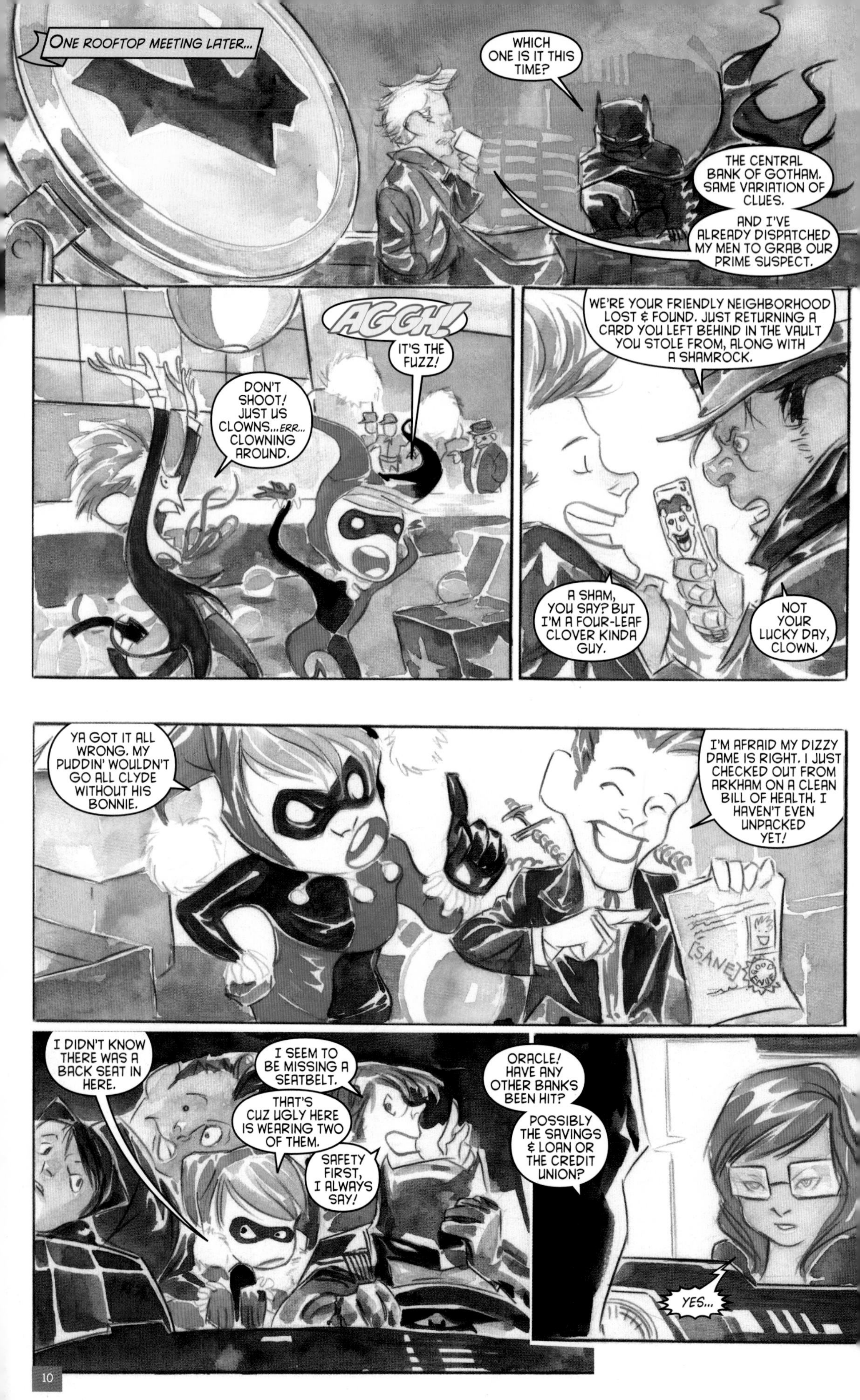
ONE ROOFTOP MEETING LATER...
WHICH ONE IS IT THIS TIME?
THE CENTRAL BANK OF GOTHAM. SAME VARIATION OF CLUES.
AND I'VE ALREADY DISPATCHED MY MEN TO GRAB OUR PRIME SUSPECT.
AGGH!
IT'S THE FUZZ!
DON'T SHOOT! JUST US CLOWNS...ERR... CLOWNING AROUND.
WE'RE YOUR FRIENDLY NEIGHBORHOOD LOST & FOUND. JUST RETURNING A CARD YOU LEFT BEHIND IN THE VAULT YOU STOLE FROM, ALONG WITH A SHAMROCK.
A SHAM, YOU SAY? BUT I'M A FOUR-LEAF CLOVER KINDA GUY.
NOT YOUR LUCKY DAY, CLOWN.
YA GOT IT ALL WRONG. MY PUDDIN' WOULDN'T GO ALL CLYDE WITHOUT HIS BONNIE.
I'M AFRAID MY DIZZY DAME IS RIGHT. I JUST CHECKED OUT FROM ARKHAM ON A CLEAN BILL OF HEALTH. I HAVEN'T EVEN UNPACKED YET!
SANE
I DIDN'T KNOW THERE WAS A BACK SEAT IN HERE.
I SEEM TO BE MISSING A SEATBELT.
THAT'S CUZ UGLY HERE IS WEARING TWO OF THEM.
SAFETY FIRST, I ALWAYS SAY!
ORACLE! HAVE ANY OTHER BANKS BEEN HIT?
POSSIBLY THE SAVINGS & LOAN OR THE CREDIT UNION?
YES...

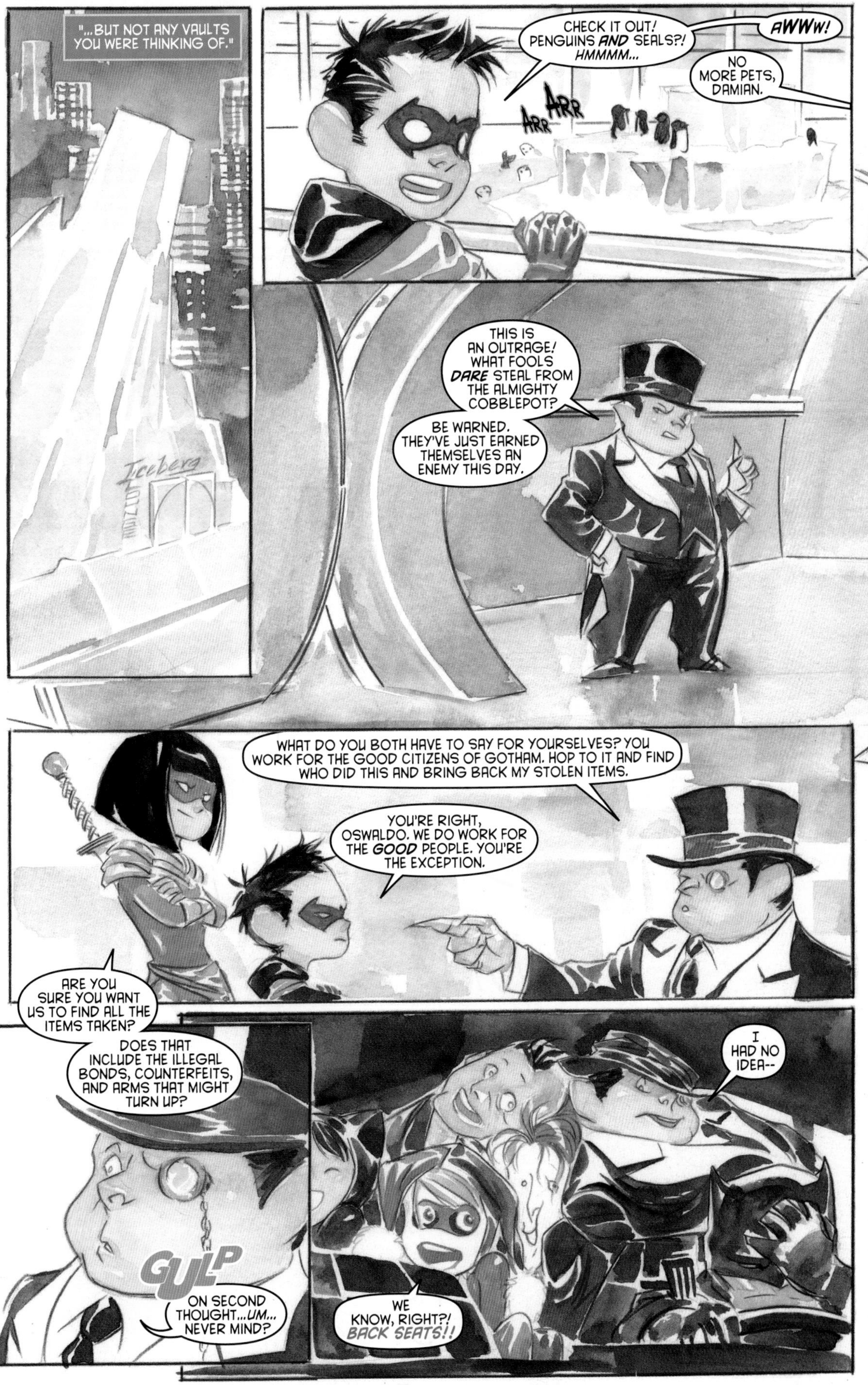

"...BUT NOT ANY VAULTS YOU WERE THINKING OF."
Iceberg
CHECK IT OUT! PENGUINS AND SEALS?! HMMMM...
AWWW!
NO MORE PETS, DAMIAN.
ARR ARR
THIS IS AN OUTRAGE! WHAT FOOLS DARE STEAL FROM THE ALMIGHTY COBBLEPOT?
BE WARNED. THEY'VE JUST EARNED THEMSELVES AN ENEMY THIS DAY.
WHAT DO YOU BOTH HAVE TO SAY FOR YOURSELVES? YOU WORK FOR THE GOOD CITIZENS OF GOTHAM. HOP TO IT AND FIND WHO DID THIS AND BRING BACK MY STOLEN ITEMS.
YOU'RE RIGHT, OSWALDO. WE DO WORK FOR THE GOOD PEOPLE. YOU'RE THE EXCEPTION.
ARE YOU SURE YOU WANT US TO FIND ALL THE ITEMS TAKEN?
DOES THAT INCLUDE THE ILLEGAL BONDS, COUNTERFEITS, AND ARMS THAT MIGHT TURN UP?
GULP
ON SECOND THOUGHT...UM... NEVER MIND?
I HAD NO IDEA--
WE KNOW, RIGHT?! BACK SEATS!!

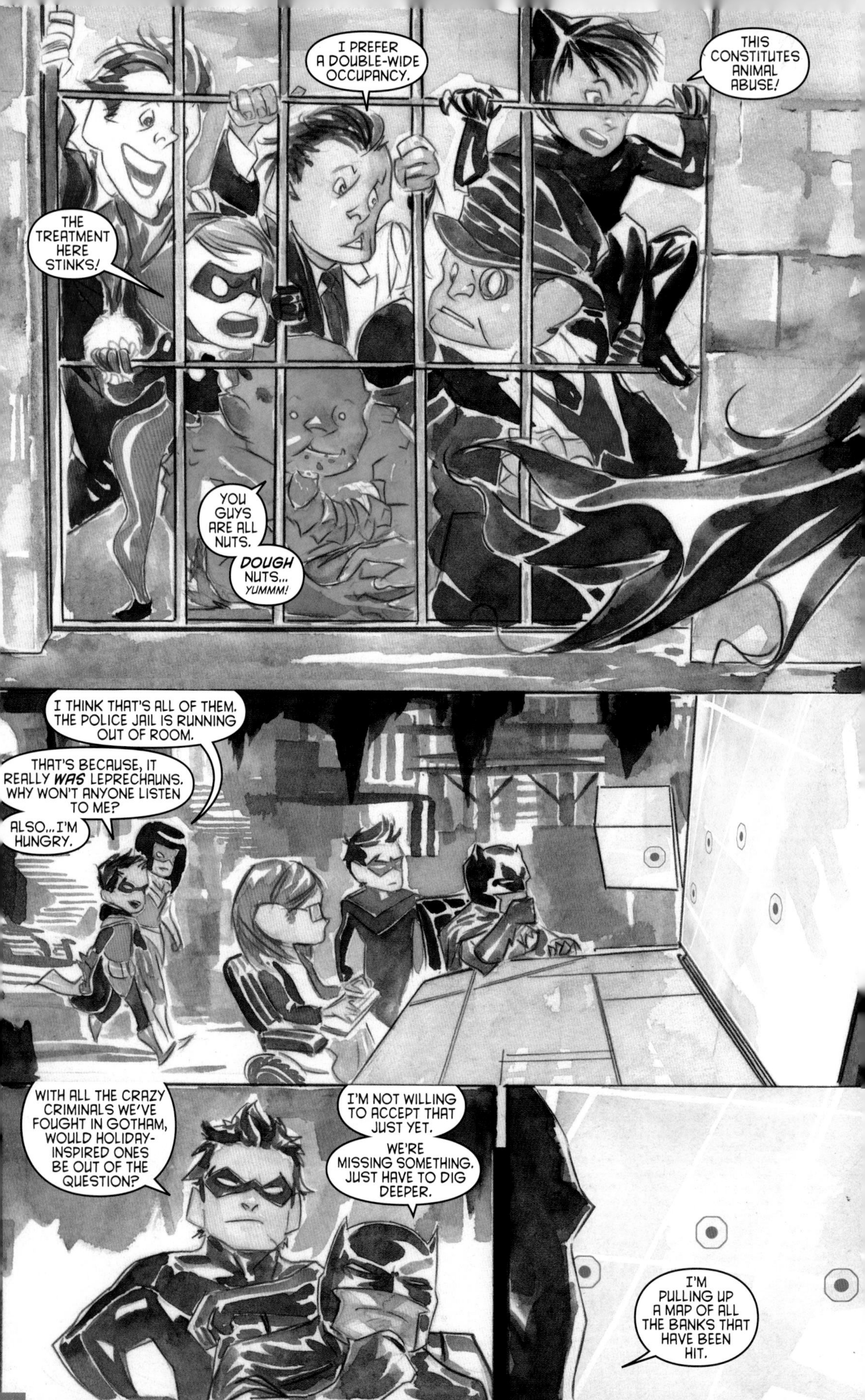
I PREFER A DOUBLE-WIDE OCCUPANCY.
THIS CONSTITUTES ANIMAL ABUSE!
THE TREATMENT HERE STINKS!
YOU GUYS ARE ALL NUTS.
DOUGH NUTS... YUMMM!
I THINK THAT'S ALL OF THEM. THE POLICE JAIL IS RUNNING OUT OF ROOM.
THAT'S BECAUSE, IT REALLY WAS LEPRECHAUNS. WHY WON'T ANYONE LISTEN TO ME?
ALSO... I'M HUNGRY.
WITH ALL THE CRAZY CRIMINALS WE'VE FOUGHT IN GOTHAM, WOULD HOLIDAY-INSPIRED ONES BE OUT OF THE QUESTION?
I'M NOT WILLING TO ACCEPT THAT JUST YET.
WE'RE MISSING SOMETHING. JUST HAVE TO DIG DEEPER.
I'M PULLING UP A MAP OF ALL THE BANKS THAT HAVE BEEN HIT.

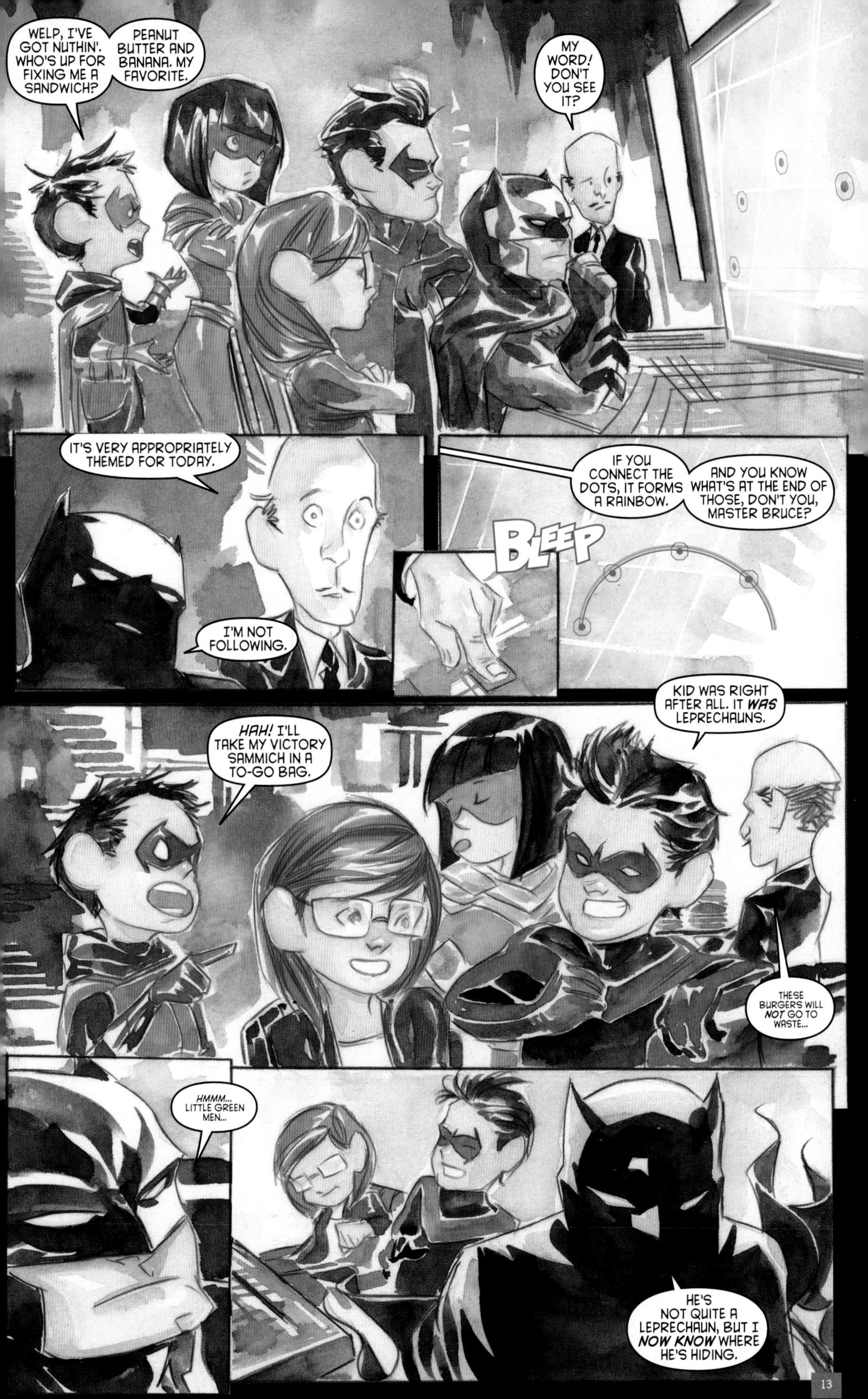
WELP, I'VE GOT NUTHIN'. WHO'S UP FOR FIXING ME A SANDWICH?
PEANUT BUTTER AND BANANA. MY FAVORITE.
MY WORD! DON'T YOU SEE IT?
IT'S VERY APPROPRIATELY THEMED FOR TODAY.
I'M NOT FOLLOWING.
IF YOU CONNECT THE DOTS, IT FORMS A RAINBOW.
AND YOU KNOW WHAT'S AT THE END OF THOSE, DON'T YOU, MASTER BRUCE?
BLEEP
HAH! I'LL TAKE MY VICTORY SAMMICH IN A TO-GO BAG.
KID WAS RIGHT AFTER ALL. IT WAS LEPRECHAUNS.
THESE BURGERS WILL NOT GO TO WASTE...
HMMM... LITTLE GREEN MEN...
HE'S NOT QUITE A LEPRECHAUN, BUT I NOW KNOW WHERE HE'S HIDING.

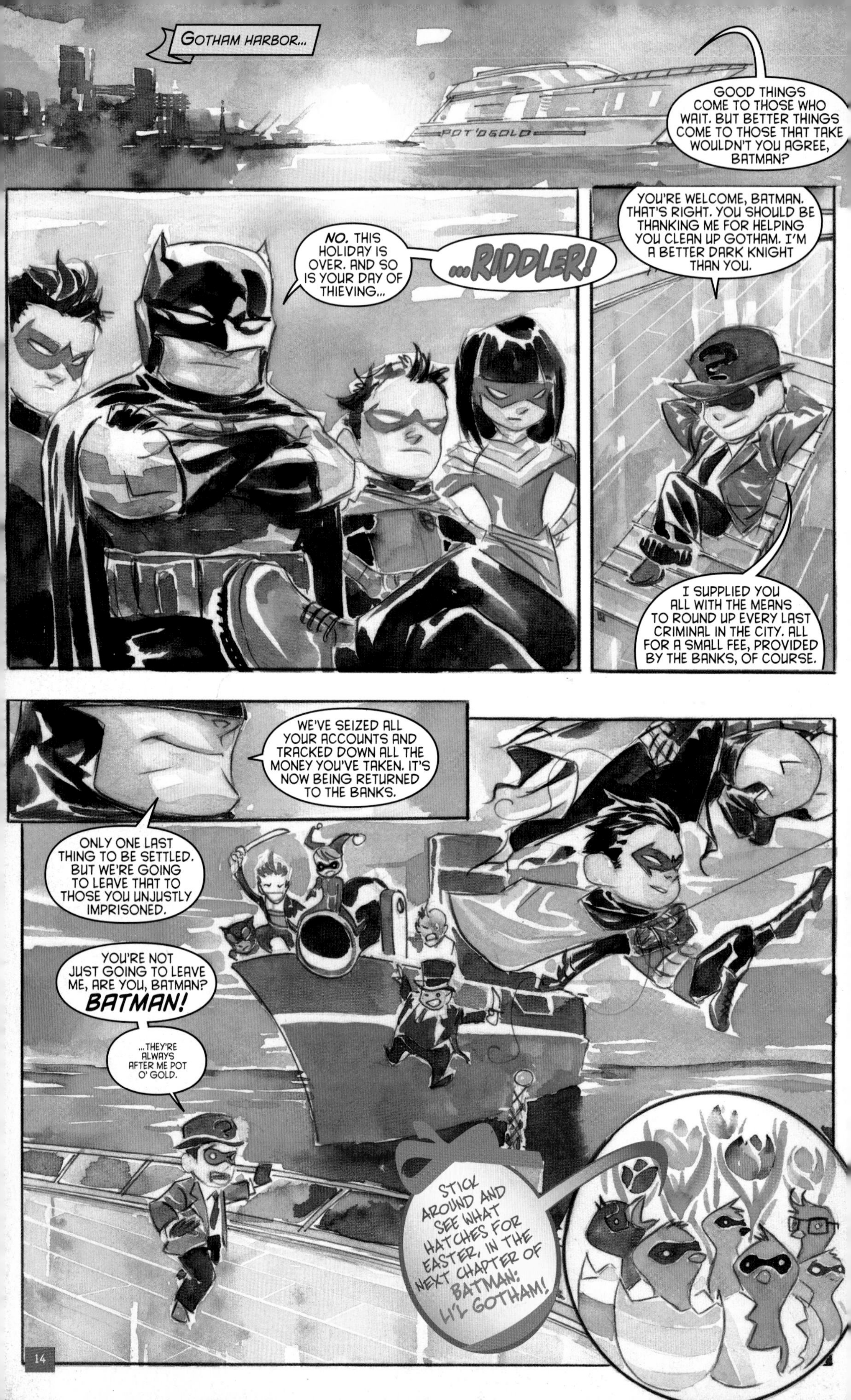

GOTHAM HARBOR...
POT 'O GOLD
GOOD THINGS COME TO THOSE WHO WAIT. BUT BETTER THINGS COME TO THOSE THAT TAKE WOULDN'T YOU AGREE, BATMAN?
NO. THIS HOLIDAY IS OVER. AND SO IS YOUR DAY OF THIEVING...
...RIDDLER!
YOU'RE WELCOME, BATMAN. THAT'S RIGHT. YOU SHOULD BE THANKING ME FOR HELPING YOU CLEAN UP GOTHAM. I'M A BETTER DARK KNIGHT THAN YOU.
I SUPPLIED YOU ALL WITH THE MEANS TO ROUND UP EVERY LAST CRIMINAL IN THE CITY. ALL FOR A SMALL FEE, PROVIDED BY THE BANKS, OF COURSE.
WE'VE SEIZED ALL YOUR ACCOUNTS AND TRACKED DOWN ALL THE MONEY YOU'VE TAKEN. IT'S NOW BEING RETURNED TO THE BANKS.
ONLY ONE LAST THING TO BE SETTLED. BUT WE'RE GOING TO LEAVE THAT TO THOSE YOU UNJUSTLY IMPRISONED.
YOU'RE NOT JUST GOING TO LEAVE ME, ARE YOU, BATMAN? BATMAN!
...THEY'RE ALWAYS AFTER ME POT O' GOLD.
STICK AROUND AND SEE WHAT HATCHES FOR EASTER, IN THE NEXT CHAPTER OF BATMAN: LI'L GOTHAM!

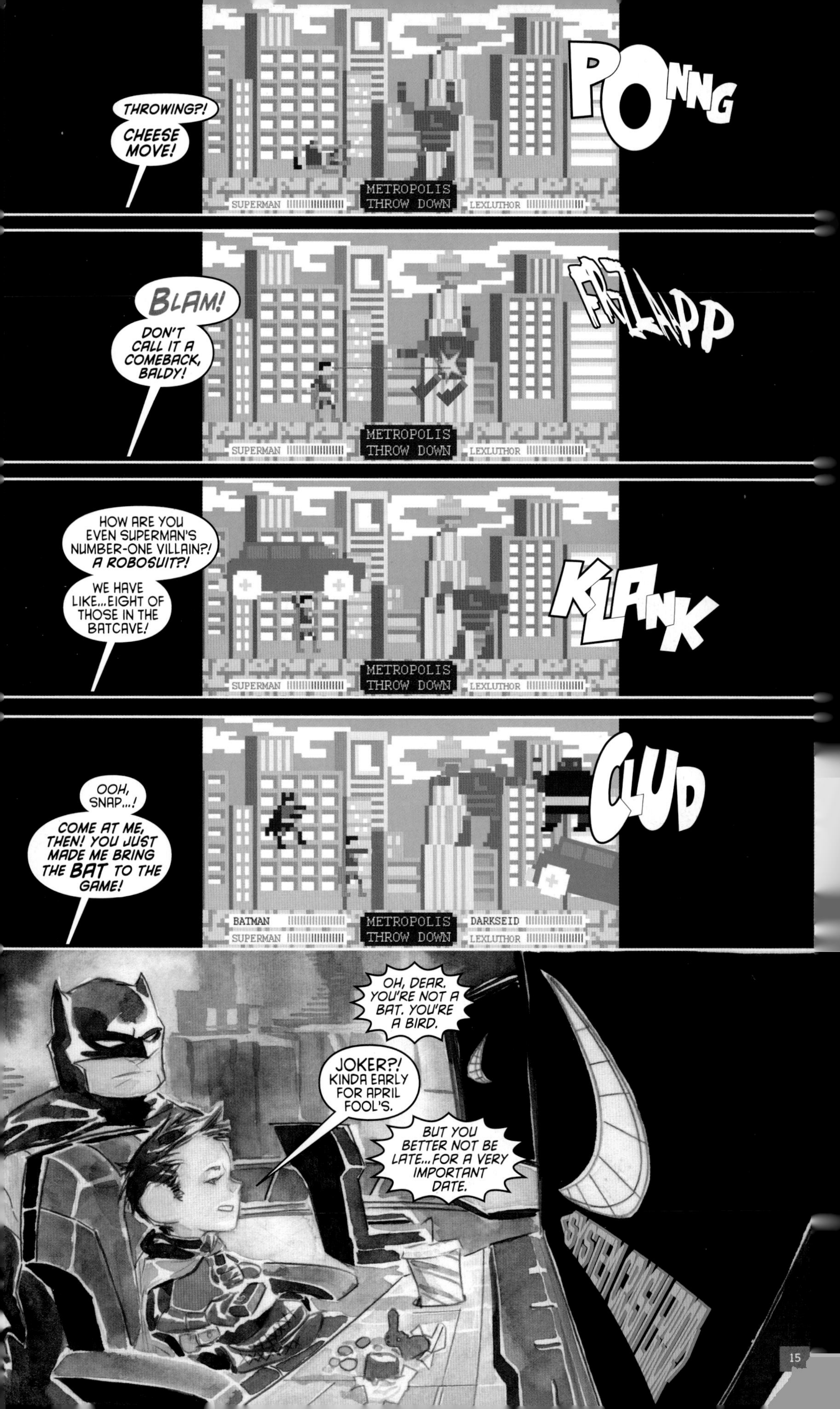
THROWING?!
CHEESE MOVE!
METROPOLIS THROW DOWN
SUPERMAN
LEXLUTHOR
PONNG
BLAM!
DON'T CALL IT A COMEBACK, BALDY!
METROPOLIS THROW DOWN
SUPERMAN
LEXLUTHOR
FRZLAAPP
HOW ARE YOU EVEN SUPERMAN'S NUMBER-ONE VILLAIN?! A ROBOSUIT?!
WE HAVE LIKE...EIGHT OF THOSE IN THE BATCAVE!
METROPOLIS THROW DOWN
SUPERMAN
LEXLUTHOR
KLANK
OOH, SNAP...!
COME AT ME, THEN! YOU JUST MADE ME BRING THE BAT TO THE GAME!
BATMAN
DARKSEID
METROPOLIS THROW DOWN
SUPERMAN
LEXLUTHOR
CLUD
OH, DEAR. YOU'RE NOT A BAT. YOU'RE A BIRD.
JOKER?! KINDA EARLY FOR APRIL FOOL'S.
BUT YOU BETTER NOT BE LATE...FOR A VERY IMPORTANT DATE.
SYSTEM CRASH

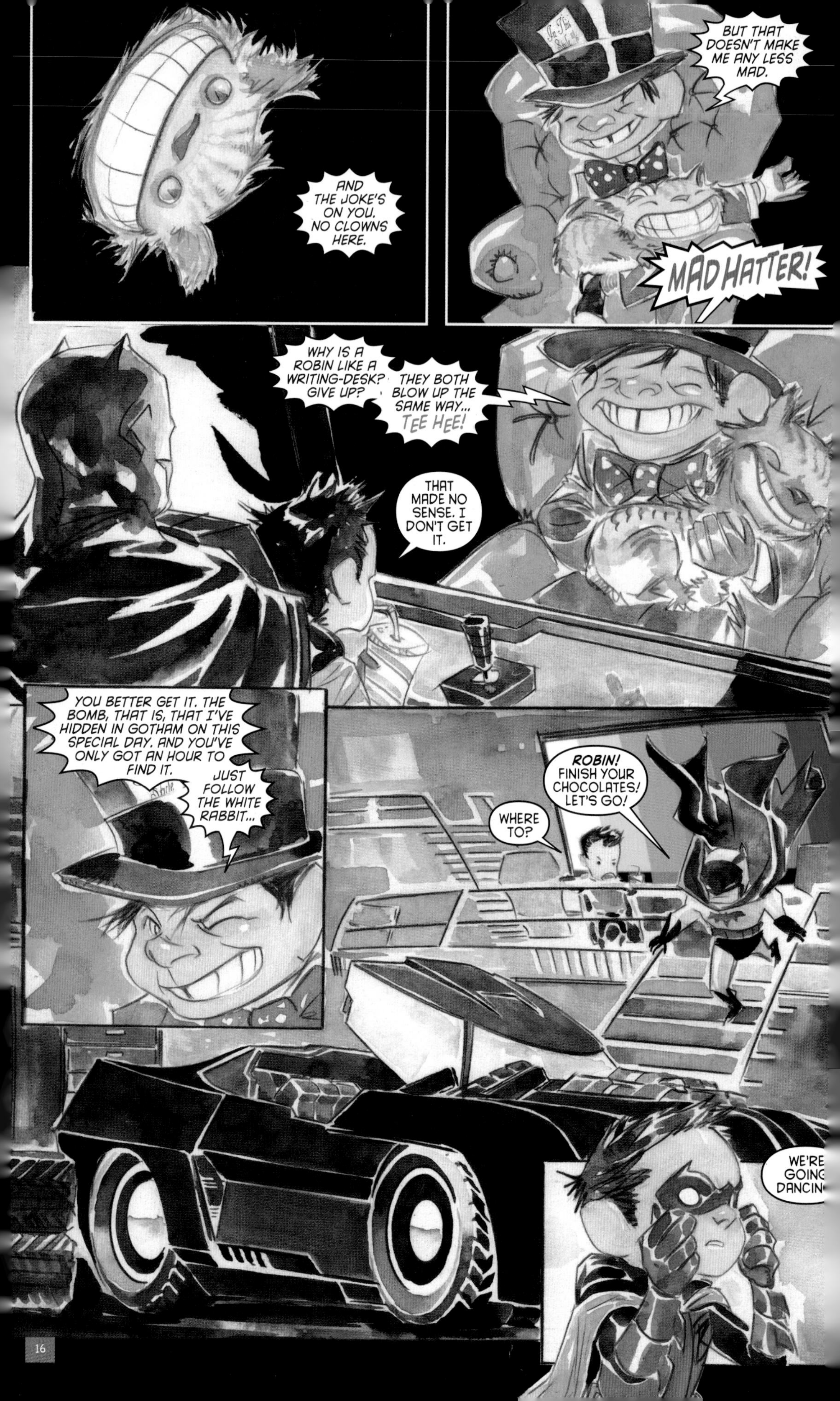

AND THE JOKE'S ON YOU. NO CLOWNS HERE.
BUT THAT DOESN'T MAKE ME ANY LESS MAD.
MAD HATTER!
WHY IS A ROBIN LIKE A WRITING-DESK? GIVE UP?
THEY BOTH BLOW UP THE SAME WAY... TEE HEE!
THAT MADE NO SENSE. I DON'T GET IT.
YOU BETTER GET IT. THE BOMB, THAT IS, THAT I'VE HIDDEN IN GOTHAM ON THIS SPECIAL DAY. AND YOU'VE ONLY GOT AN HOUR TO FIND IT.
JUST FOLLOW THE WHITE RABBIT...
ROBIN! FINISH YOUR CHOCOLATES! LET'S GO!
WHERE TO?
WE'RE GOING DANCIN

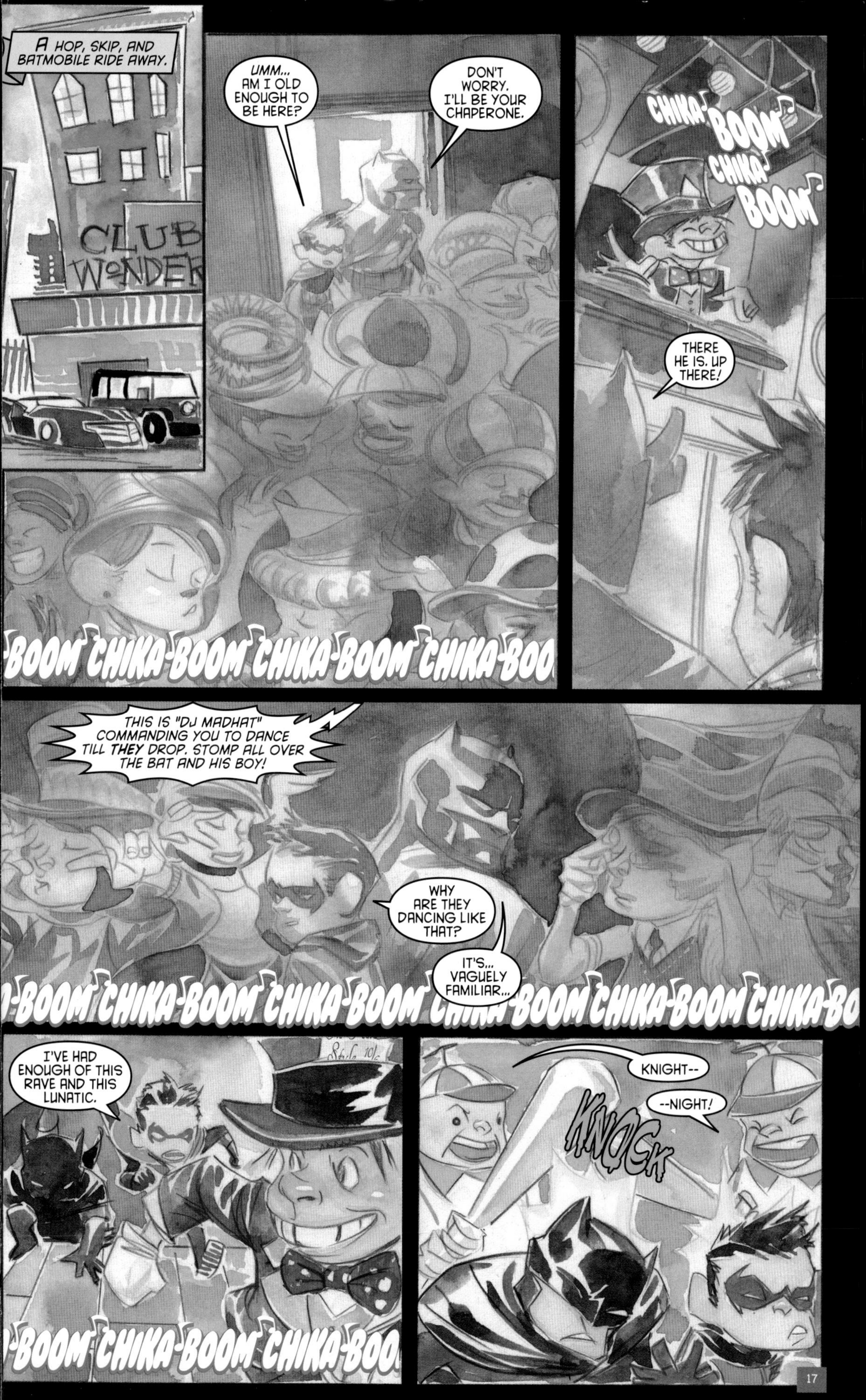
A HOP, SKIP, AND BATMOBILE RIDE AWAY.
CLUB WONDER
UMM... AM I OLD ENOUGH TO BE HERE?
DON'T WORRY. I'LL BE YOUR CHAPERONE.
-BOOM CHIKA-BOOM CHIKA-BOOM CHIKA-BOO
CHIKA-BOOM CHIKA-BOOM
THERE HE IS. UP THERE!
THIS IS "DJ MADHAT" COMMANDING YOU TO DANCE TILL THEY DROP. STOMP ALL OVER THE BAT AND HIS BOY!
WHY ARE THEY DANCING LIKE THAT?
IT'S... VAGUELY FAMILIAR...
-BOOM CHIKA-BOOM CHIKA-BOOM CHIKA-BOOM CHIKA-BOOM CHIKA-BO
I'VE HAD ENOUGH OF THIS RAVE AND THIS LUNATIC.
-BOOM CHIKA-BOOM CHIKA-BOO
KNIGHT--
--NIGHT!
KNOCK

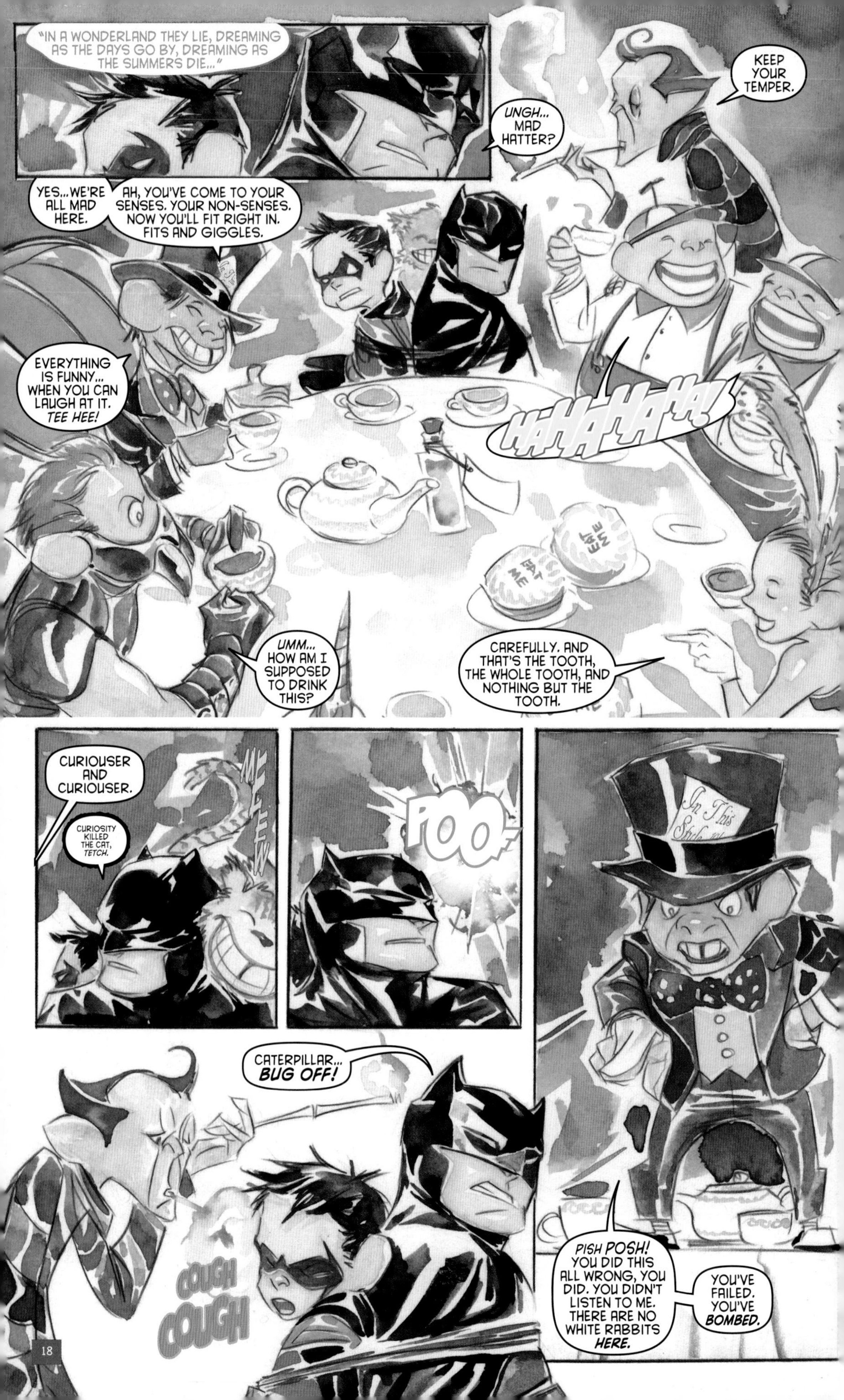
"IN A WONDERLAND THEY LIE, DREAMING AS THE DAYS GO BY, DREAMING AS THE SUMMERS DIE..."
UNGH... MAD HATTER?
KEEP YOUR TEMPER.
YES...WE'RE ALL MAD HERE.
AH, YOU'VE COME TO YOUR SENSES. YOUR NON-SENSES. NOW YOU'LL FIT RIGHT IN. FITS AND GIGGLES.
EVERYTHING IS FUNNY... WHEN YOU CAN LAUGH AT IT. TEE HEE!
HAHAHAHA!
EAT ME
EAT ME
UMM... HOW AM I SUPPOSED TO DRINK THIS?
CAREFULLY. AND THAT'S THE TOOTH, THE WHOLE TOOTH, AND NOTHING BUT THE TOOTH.
CURIOUSER AND CURIOUSER.
CURIOSITY KILLED THE CAT, TETCH.
MEEEW
POOF
In This Style
CATERPILLAR... BUG OFF!
COUGH COUGH
PISH POSH! YOU DID THIS ALL WRONG, YOU DID. YOU DIDN'T LISTEN TO ME. THERE ARE NO WHITE RABBITS HERE.
YOU'VE FAILED. YOU'VE BOMBED.

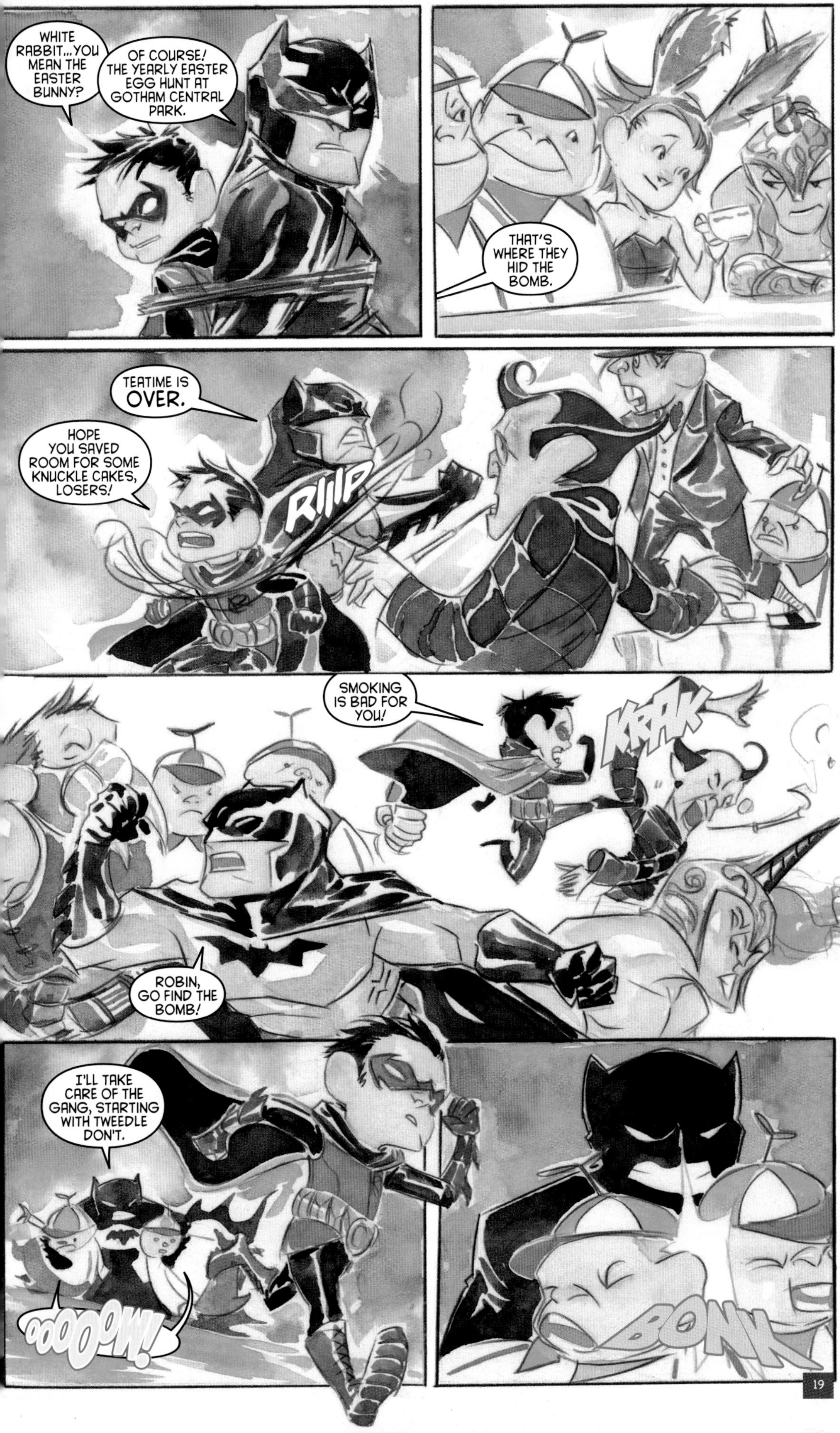
WHITE RABBIT...YOU MEAN THE EASTER BUNNY?
OF COURSE! THE YEARLY EASTER EGG HUNT AT GOTHAM CENTRAL PARK.
THAT'S WHERE THEY HID THE BOMB.
TEATIME IS OVER.
HOPE YOU SAVED ROOM FOR SOME KNUCKLE CAKES, LOSERS!
RIIIP
SMOKING IS BAD FOR YOU!
KRAK
ROBIN, GO FIND THE BOMB!
I'LL TAKE CARE OF THE GANG, STARTING WITH TWEEDLE DON'T.
OOOOOOM!
BONK

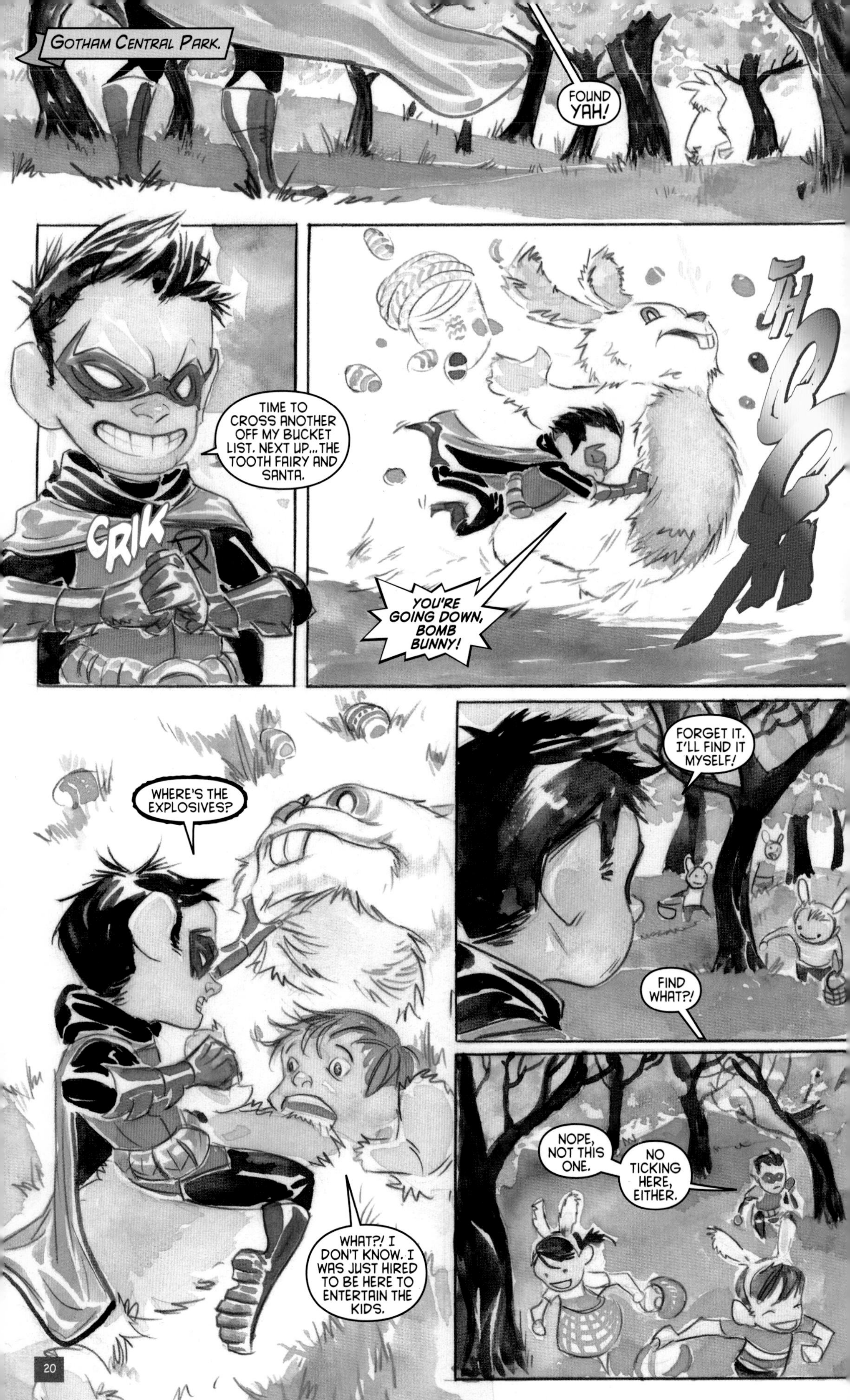
GOTHAM CENTRAL PARK.
FOUND YAH!
TIME TO CROSS ANOTHER OFF MY BUCKET LIST. NEXT UP... THE TOOTH FAIRY AND SANTA.
CRIK
YOU'RE GOING DOWN, BOMB BUNNY!
WHERE'S THE EXPLOSIVES?
WHAT?! I DON'T KNOW. I WAS JUST HIRED TO BE HERE TO ENTERTAIN THE KIDS.
FORGET IT. I'LL FIND IT MYSELF!
FIND WHAT?!
NOPE, NOT THIS ONE.
NO TICKING HERE, EITHER.

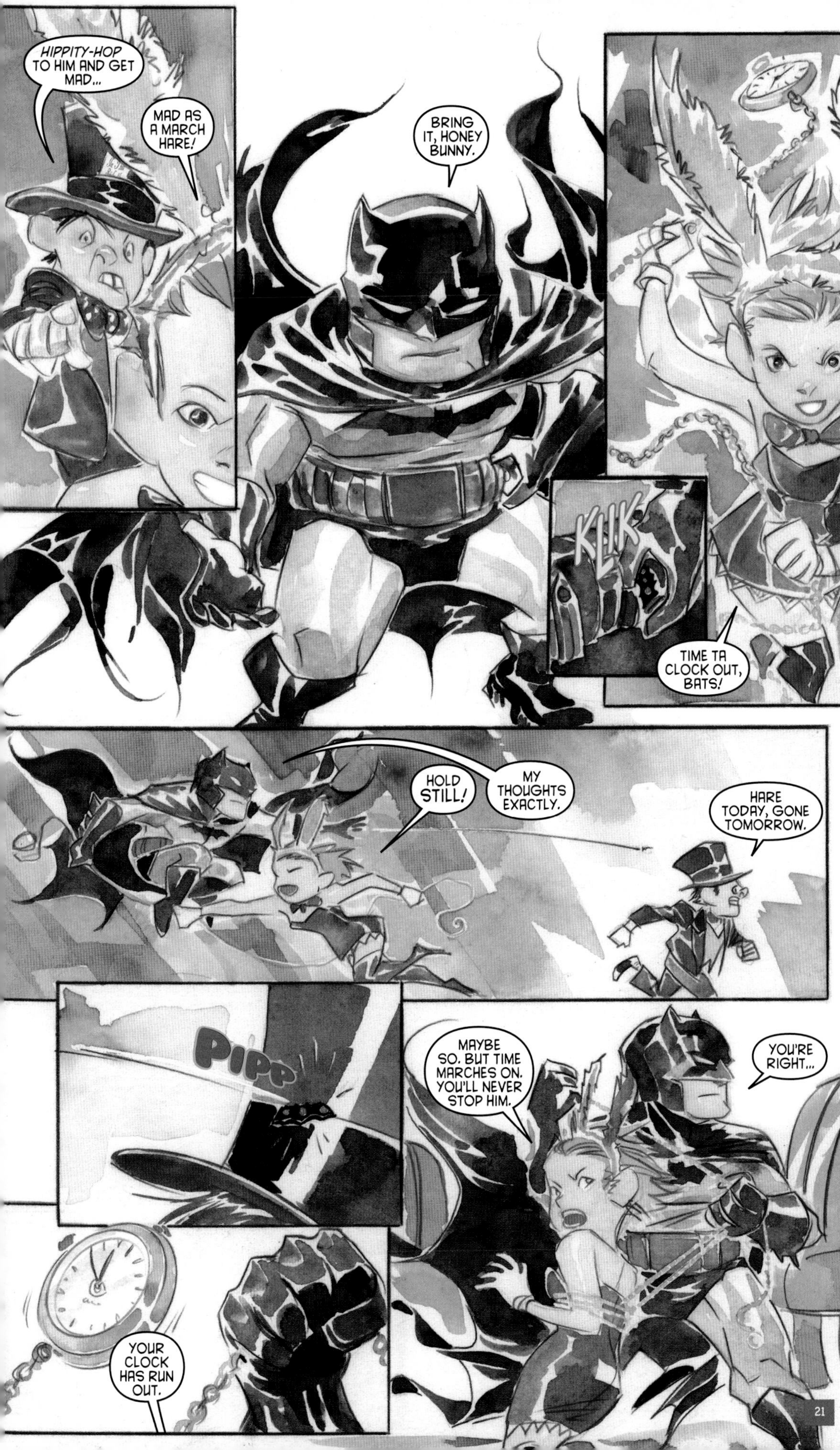
HIPPITY-HOP TO HIM AND GET MAD...
MAD AS A MARCH HARE!
BRING IT, HONEY BUNNY.
KLIK
TIME TA CLOCK OUT, BATS!
HOLD STILL!
MY THOUGHTS EXACTLY.
HARE TODAY, GONE TOMORROW.
PIPP
MAYBE SO. BUT TIME MARCHES ON. YOU'LL NEVER STOP HIM.
YOU'RE RIGHT...
YOUR CLOCK HAS RUN OUT.

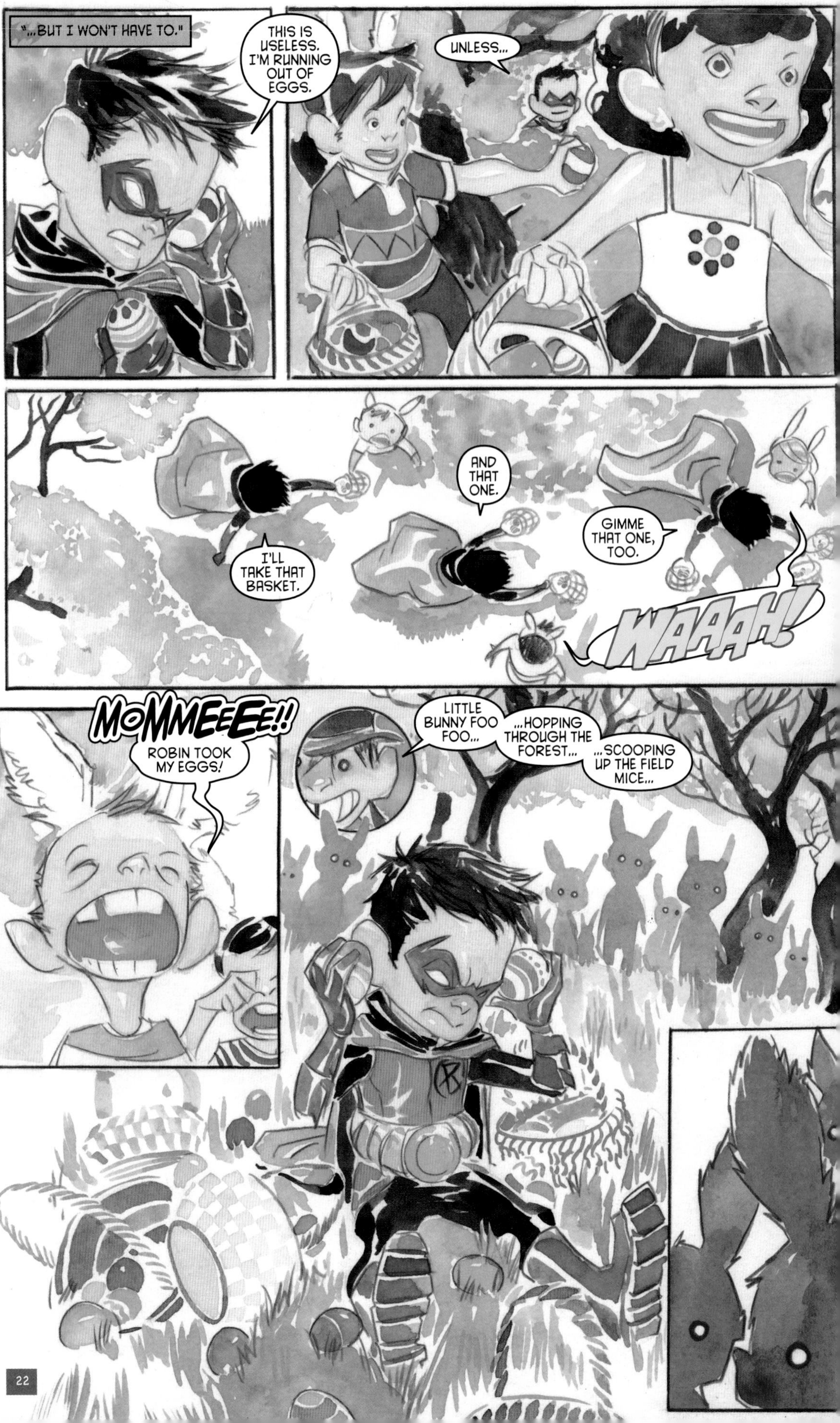
"...BUT I WON'T HAVE TO."
THIS IS USELESS. I'M RUNNING OUT OF EGGS.
UNLESS...
AND THAT ONE.
I'LL TAKE THAT BASKET.
GIMME THAT ONE, TOO.
WAAAH!
MOMMEEEEE!!
ROBIN TOOK MY EGGS!
LITTLE BUNNY FOO FOO...
...HOPPING THROUGH THE FOREST...
...SCOOPING UP THE FIELD MICE...

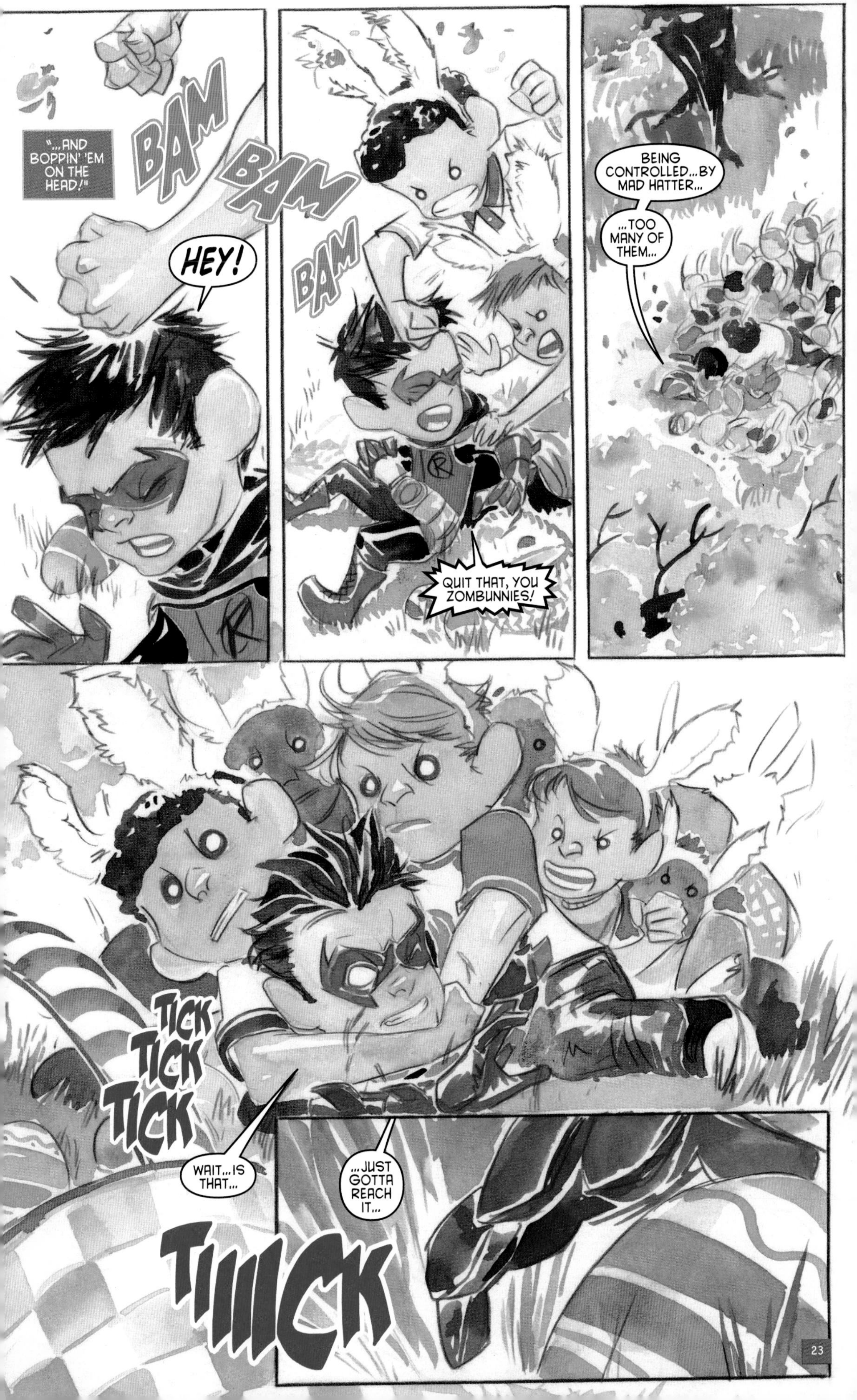
"...AND BOPPIN' 'EM ON THE HEAD!"
BAM
HEY!
BAM
BAM
QUIT THAT, YOU ZOMBUNNIES!
BEING CONTROLLED...BY MAD HATTER...
...TOO MANY OF THEM...
TICK TICK TICK
WAIT...IS THAT...
...JUST GOTTA REACH IT...
TIIIICK

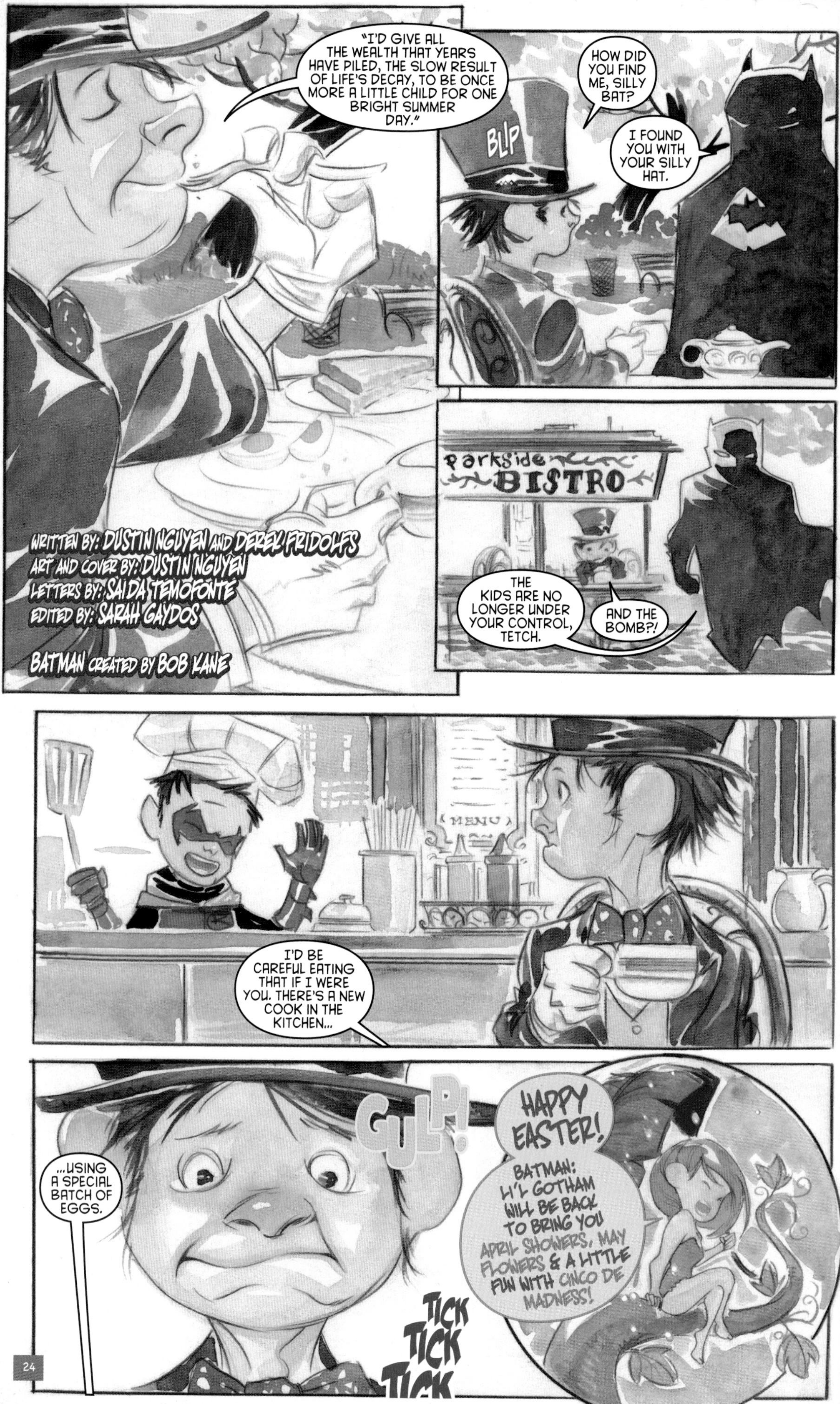
"I'D GIVE ALL THE WEALTH THAT YEARS HAVE PILED, THE SLOW RESULT OF LIFE'S DECAY, TO BE ONCE MORE A LITTLE CHILD FOR ONE BRIGHT SUMMER DAY."
WRITTEN BY: DUSTIN NGUYEN AND DEREK FRIDOLFS
ART AND COVER BY: DUSTIN NGUYEN
LETTERS BY: SAIDA TEMOFONTE
EDITED BY: SARAH GAYDOS
BATMAN CREATED BY BOB KANE
BLIP
HOW DID YOU FIND ME, SILLY BAT?
I FOUND YOU WITH YOUR SILLY HAT.
PARKSIDE BISTRO
THE KIDS ARE NO LONGER UNDER YOUR CONTROL, TETCH.
AND THE BOMB?!
MENU
I'D BE CAREFUL EATING THAT IF I WERE YOU. THERE'S A NEW COOK IN THE KITCHEN...
GULP!
...USING A SPECIAL BATCH OF EGGS.
HAPPY EASTER!
BATMAN: LI'L GOTHAM WILL BE BACK TO BRING YOU APRIL SHOWERS, MAY FLOWERS & A LITTLE FUN WITH CINCO DE MADNESS!
TICK
TICK
TICK

CREATORS

DUSTIN NGUYEN — CO-WRITER & ILLUSTRATOR

Dustin Nguyen is an American comic artist whose body of work includes Wildcats v3.0, The Authority Revolution, Batman, Superman/Batman, Detective Comics, Batgirl, and his creator owned project Manifest Eternity. Currently, he produces all the art for Batman: Li'l Gotham, which is also written by himself and Derek Fridolfs. Outside of comics, Dustin moonlights as a conceptual artist for toys, games, and animation. In his spare time, he enjoys sleeping, driving, and sketching things he loves.

DEREK FRIDOLFS — CO-WRITER

Derek Fridolfs is a comic book writer, inker, and artist. He resides in Gotham--present and future.

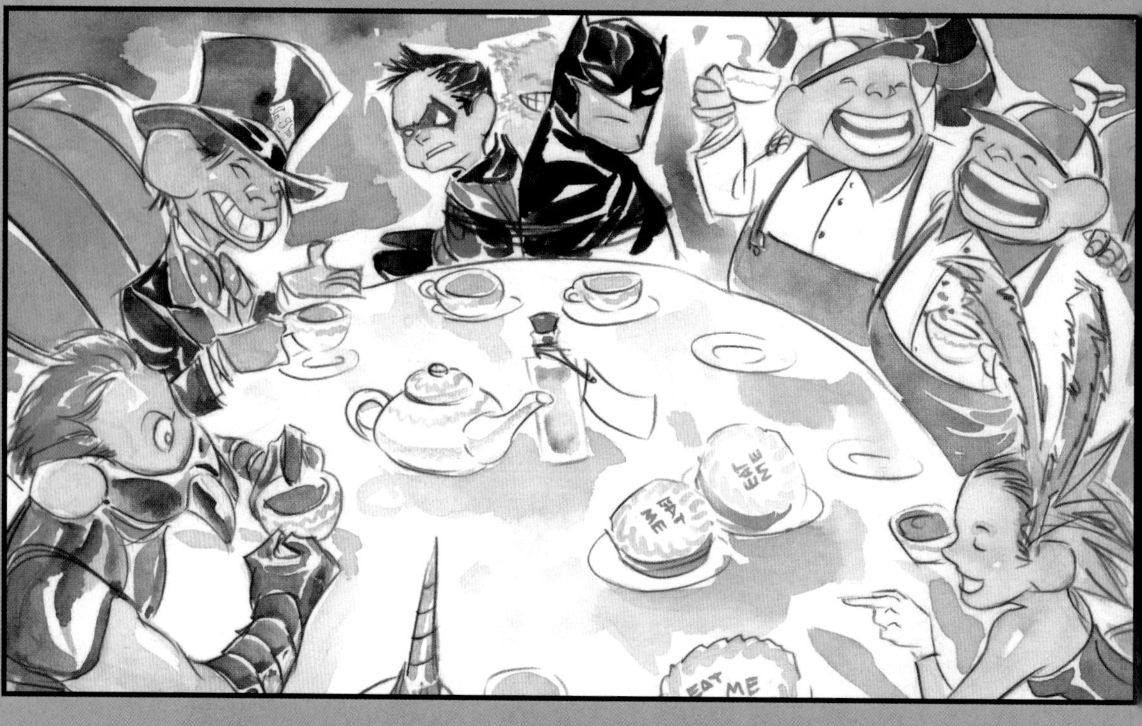
EAT ME

GLOSSARY

chaperone (SHAP-uh-rone)--a person who goes with, and is responsible for, a young person

counterfeits (KOWN-tur-fitz)--imitations or copies that are used to deceive

curiosity (kyoor-ee-OSS-uh-tee)--an eager desire to learn and often to learn what does not concern one

deceiving (di-SEEV-ing)--to cause to believe what is untrue

legit (leh-JITT)--legitimate, or for real

leprechaun (LEP-ruh-con)--a mischievous elf of Irish folklore that some believe will reveal where treasure is hidden if caught

plied (PLYED)--used or wielded steadily or forcefully

seized (SEEZD)--held forcefully or took possession of by force

shamrock (SHAM-rock)--a plant of folk legend with leaves composed of three leaflets that is associated with St. Patrick and Ireland

suspect (SUHSS-spekt)--regard with suspicion

VISUAL QUESTIONS & PROMPTS

1. What is Batman doing in these panels? What is he spraying? Why does he think Catwoman is involved?

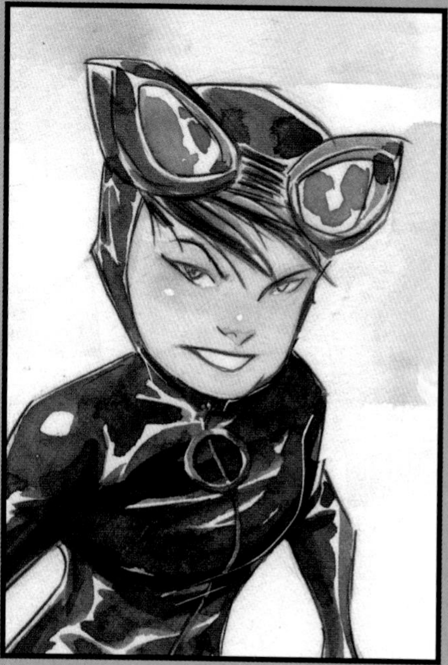

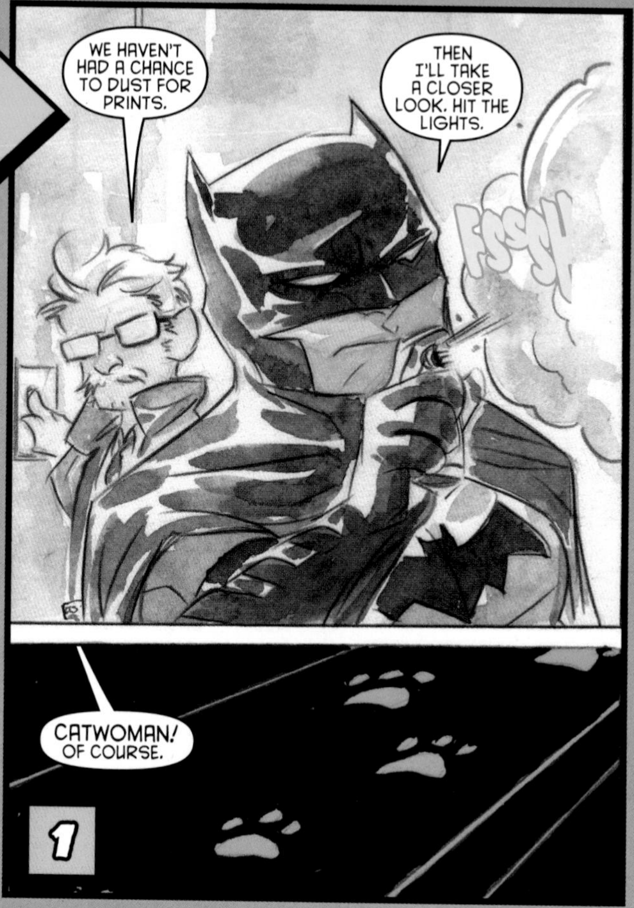

WE HAVEN'T HAD A CHANCE TO DUST FOR PRINTS.
THEN I'LL TAKE A CLOSER LOOK. HIT THE LIGHTS.
CATWOMAN! OF COURSE.
1

2. Why is Robin's word balloon pointy in this panel?

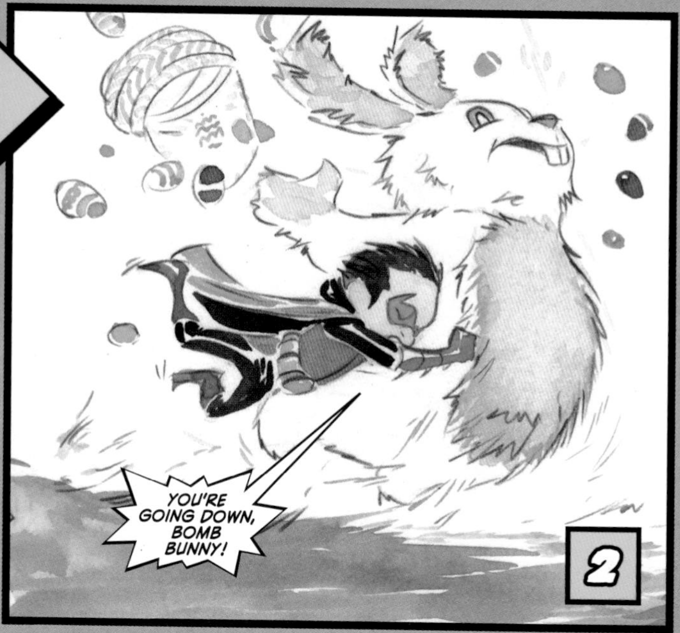

YOU'RE GOING DOWN, BOMB BUNNY!
2

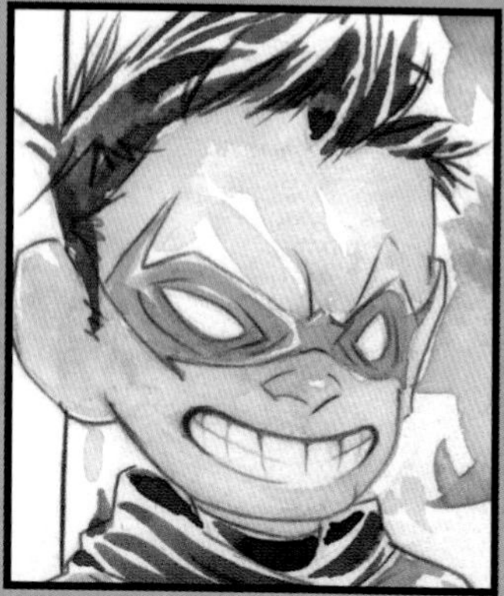

3. What is going on in these panels? Reread page 15 for clues.

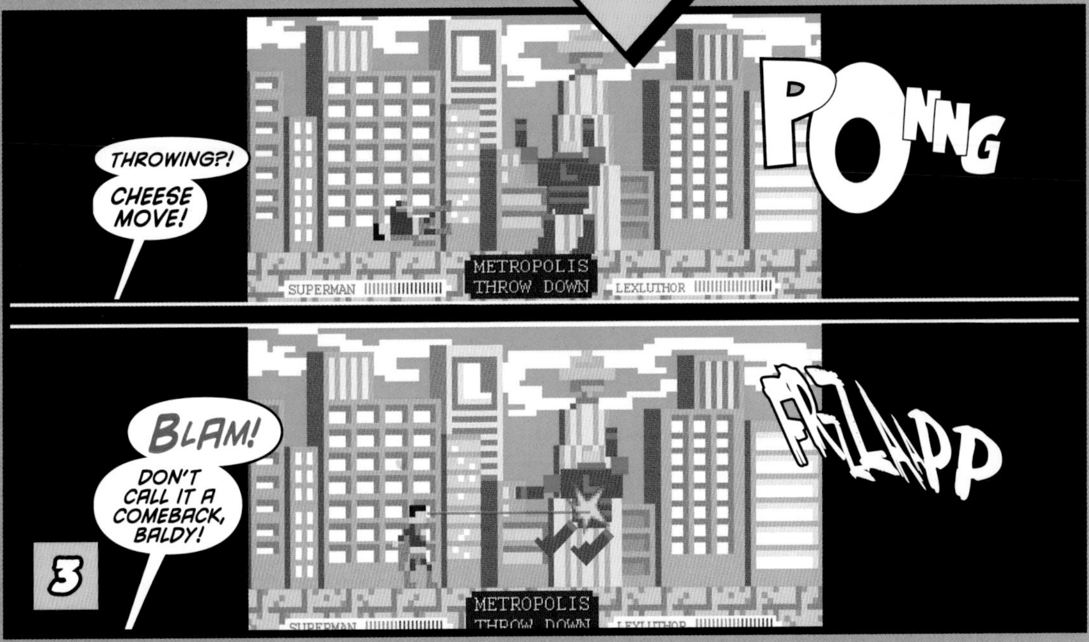
THROWING?!
CHEESE MOVE!
PONNG
METROPOLIS THROW DOWN
SUPERMAN
LEXLUTHOR
BLAM!
DON'T CALL IT A COMEBACK, BALDY!
3

4. Why is Robin hunting eggs?

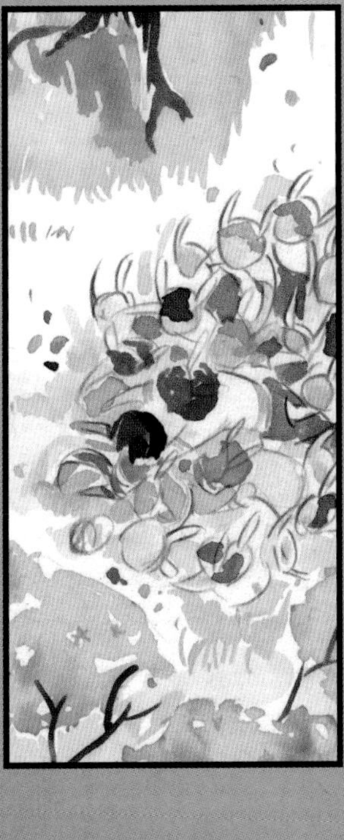

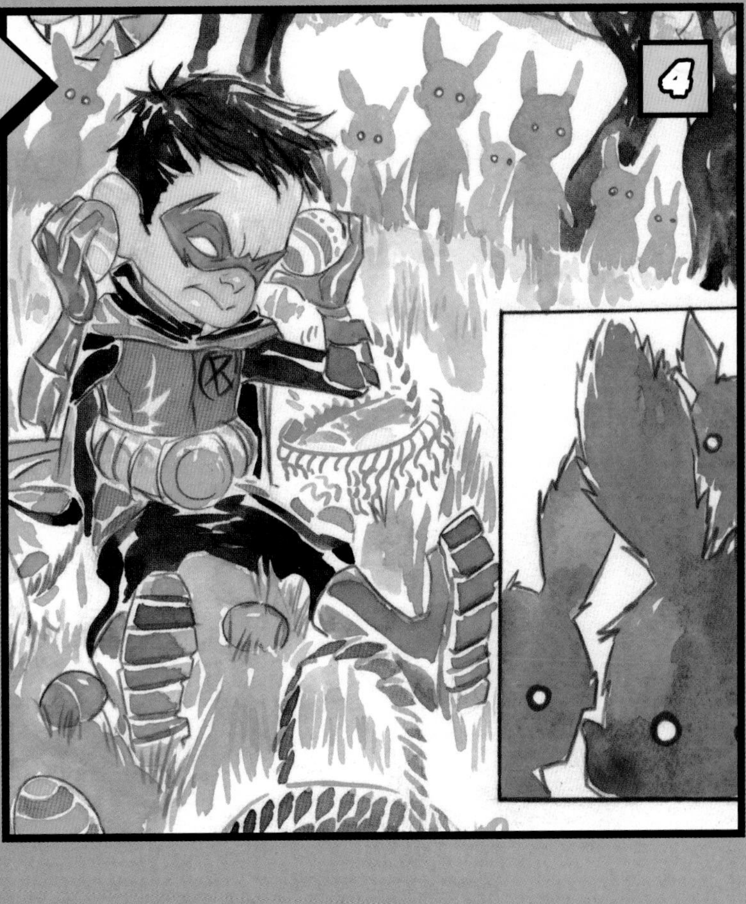
4

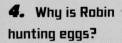

BATMAN™
LI'L GOTHAM

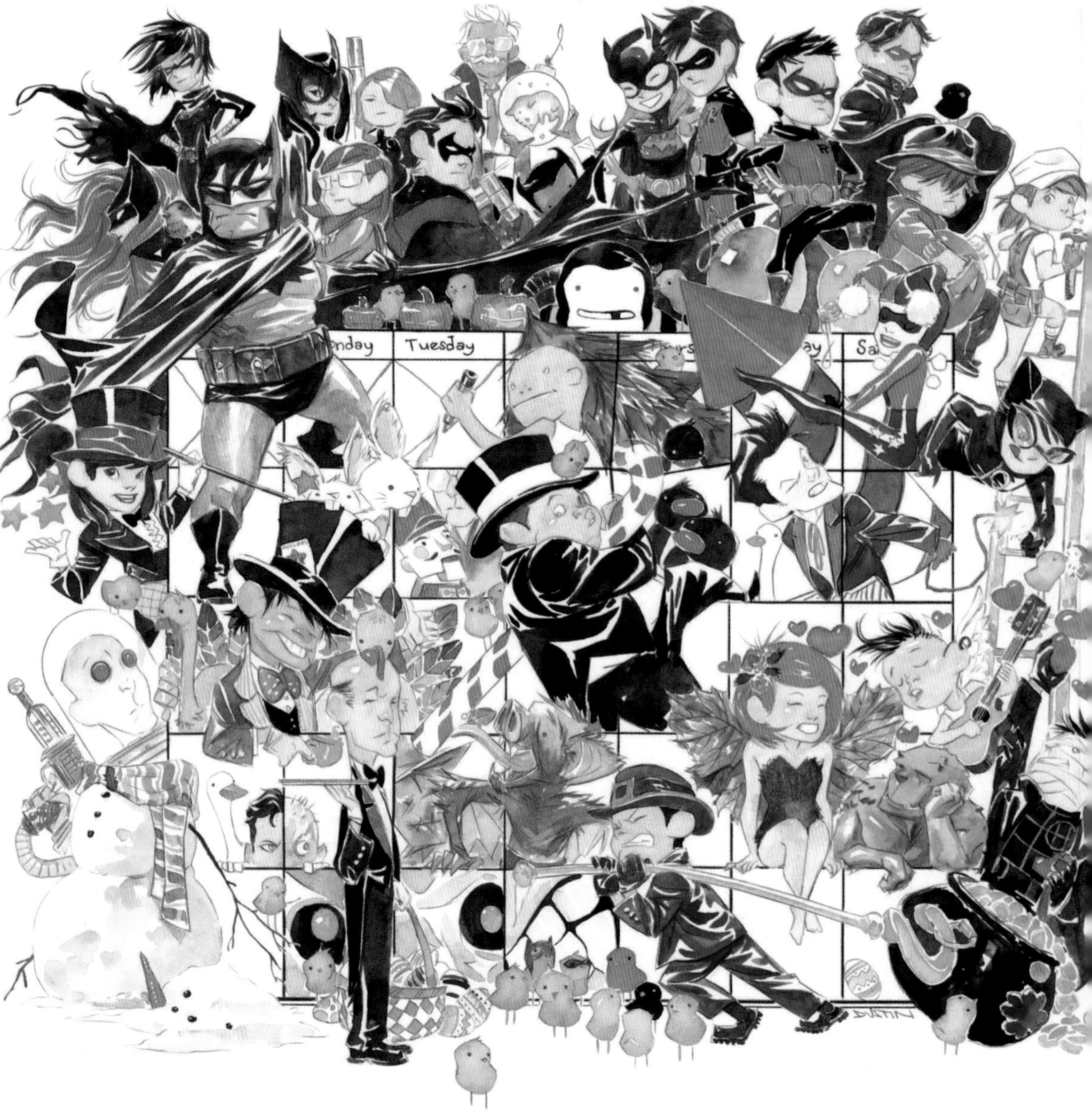

Tuesday

READ THEM ALL!

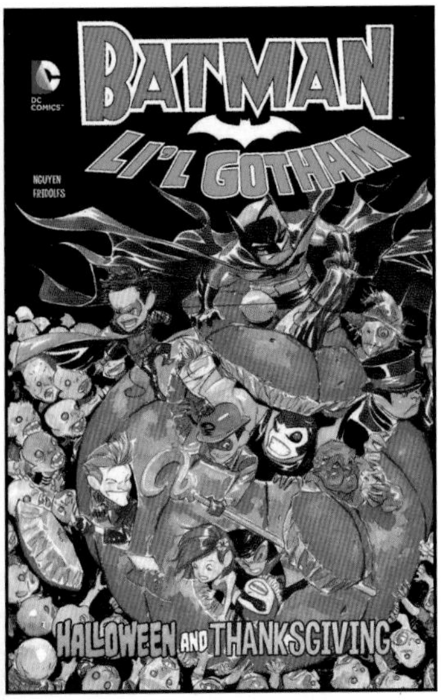
DC COMICS
BATMAN
LI'L GOTHAM
NGUYEN
FRIDOLFS
HALLOWEEN AND THANKSGIVING

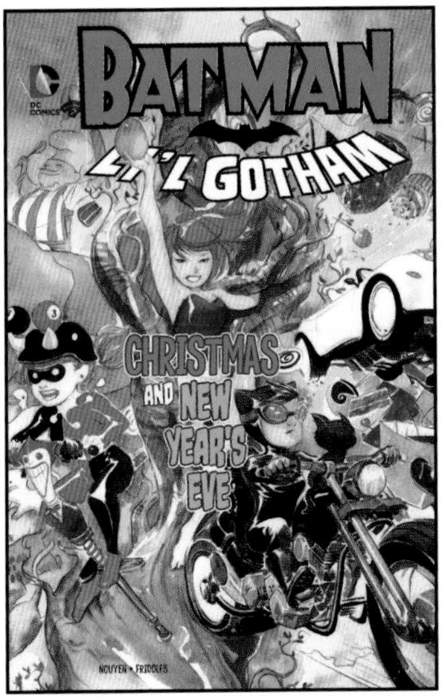
DC COMICS
BATMAN
LI'L GOTHAM
CHRISTMAS AND NEW YEAR'S EVE
NGUYEN • FRIDOLFS

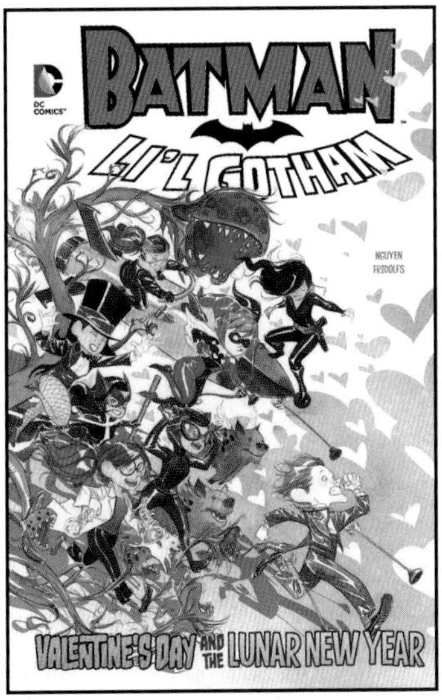
DC COMICS
BATMAN
LI'L GOTHAM
NGUYEN
FRIDOLFS
VALENTINE'S DAY AND THE LUNAR NEW YEAR

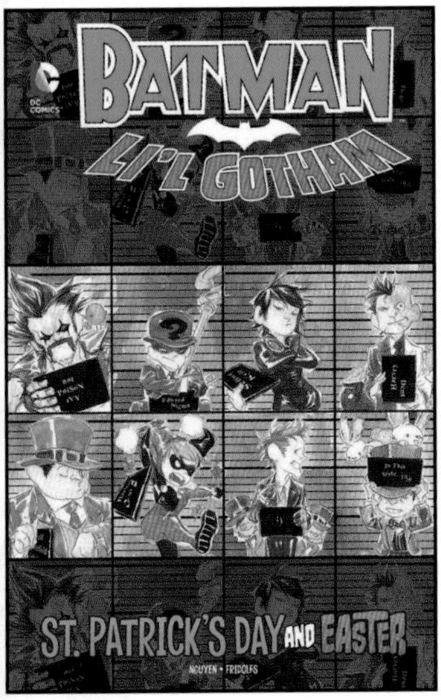
DC COMICS
BATMAN
LI'L GOTHAM
ST. PATRICK'S DAY AND EASTER
NGUYEN • FRIDOLFS

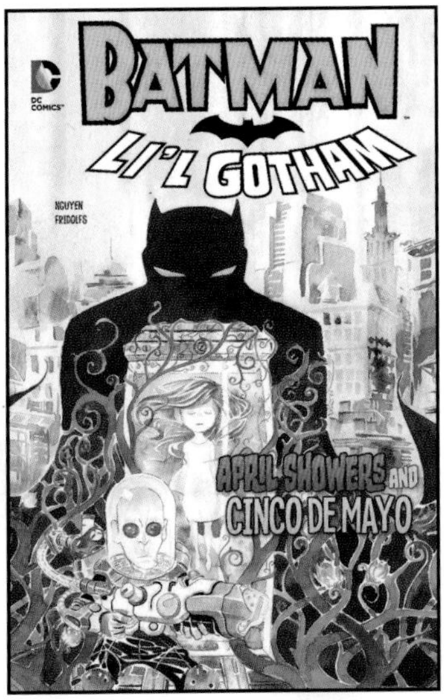
DC COMICS
BATMAN
LI'L GOTHAM
NGUYEN
FRIDOLFS
APRIL SHOWERS AND CINCO DE MAYO

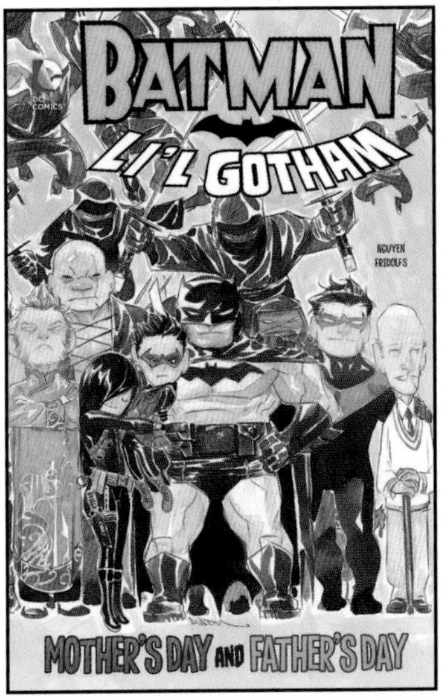
DC COMICS
BATMAN
LI'L GOTHAM
NGUYEN
FRIDOLFS
MOTHER'S DAY AND FATHER'S DAY

only from...

STONE ARCH BOOKS™
a capstone imprint www.capstonepub.com

BATMAN™
LI'L GOTHAM

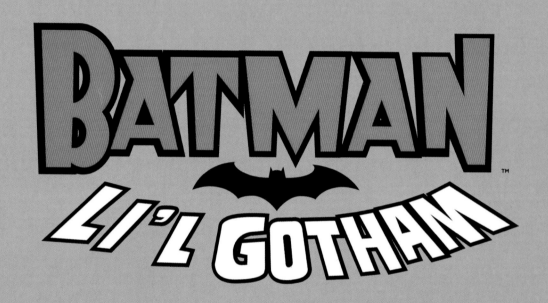